RESTLESS

Also by Rich Wallace

Losing Is Not an Option

Playing Without the Ball

Shots on Goal

Wrestling Sturbridge

RESTLESS

a ghost's story

Rich Wallace

Viking

Viking

Published by Penguin Group

Penguin Young Readers Group, 345 Hudson Street, New York, New York 10014, U.S.A.

Penguin Books Ltd, 80 Strand, London WC2R ORL, England

Penguin Books Australia Ltd, 250 Camberwell Road, Camberwell, Victoria, 3124, Australia

Penguin Books Canada Ltd, 10 Alcorn Avenue, Toronto, Ontario, Canada M4V 3B2

Penguin Books (N.Z.) Ltd, 182-190 Wairau Road, Auckland 10, New Zealand

First published in 2003 by Viking, a division of Penguin Young Readers Group

3 5 7 9 10 8 6 4 2

This is a work of fiction. The characters and events in this story
are not based on real people or events.

LIBRARY OF CONGRESS CATALOGING-IN-PUBLICATION DATA

Wallace, Rich.

Restless / Rich Wallace.

p. cm.

Summary: Frank, a teenaged ghost who has not been able to move on to a
higher realm in the afterlife, tries to connect with his younger brother Herbie,
a high school senior who was eight years old when Frank died.

ISBN 0-670-03605-6 (hardcover)

[1. Ghosts—Fiction. 2. Supernatural—Fiction. 3. Brothers—Fiction.]

I. Title.

PZ7.W15877 Re 2003   [Fic]—dc21   2003010125

Printed in U.S.A.   Set in Esprit   Book design by Nancy Brennan

For Bobby

When I'm all alone
In the great unknown,
I'll remember you.

—Bob Dylan

RESTLESS

Chapter One

I've been thinking about the undead.

Those that hover in the gap between body and spirit, clinging to the smoldering remnants of their once-living tissue, unable to float toward the light.

It's easy for most. To die, I mean. To let go. To say: That was good, this stage is done, my survivors will mourn me and remember me and continue without me. And then they'll join me on the other side when their own time arrives.

But take a man like Eamon Connelly.

Eamon made his way in 1887 from Limerick to New York to Scranton, and within a year he was loading coal onto canal boats at the town of Dyberry Forks, Pennsylvania. He was twenty-one, thin like a whip and strong. Good-hearted. Nice to dogs and children, but essentially a loner. Flat broke from drinking. Hardest-working guy on the docks.

The coal came from the Moosic Mountain mines near Scranton and traveled the same thirty-mile Sturbridge Rail Line that had brought Eamon to the Forks. From Dyberry, the coal Eamon helped load made its way via canal boat to New York, one hundred miles southeast, where several booming industries put it to use.

You can see a kind of broken symmetry in this and imagine a tiny fraction of the manufacturers' output eventually finding its way to Ireland, maybe even back to Limerick.

I wish I could say the same for Eamon.

But Eamon has never left the area once known as Dyberry Forks.

Eamon cannot see the path.

These were Eamon's final hours as walking, breathing flesh and blood.

He left the docks late that August afternoon in 1888, a few coins and one dollar bill in his pocket, and walked the three blocks to Donovan's store. He was planning to buy some tobacco. His further intention was to talk to Donovan's daughter, Gwen. Not just talk. Make contact. Warm things up a bit.

He got to the store, stood on the front step a minute, then walked the three blocks back to the docks and fortified himself with a whiskey at the Dyberry Tavern. Then he walked back to the store.

Gwen was twenty. Kept a tidy shop. Winked at Eamon when he came in, wet two fingers with her tongue, and wiped some coal dust from above Eamon's eyes.

He got his tobacco. Said it looked like rain, and maybe he'd stop back later.

"Please do," she said, giving him a sweet smile.

So he went back to the tavern and had three more whiskeys. Could still feel her fingers on his brow. Then he felt a hand on his shoulder.

Honus Wright was big. He'd sworn that very afternoon that he'd bust every bone in Eamon's skinny body for making him look bad in front of the foreman. He shoved Eamon off the stool, but Eamon was in no mood to fight. Honus said he'd kill him. The barman intervened. Eamon took a step behind two other dock workers and snuck sheepishly out the back door. They were howling with laughter as he left.

Should have stayed and fought. Would have lost another tooth, at least, but wouldn't have lost his dignity. Honus was a slacker; never pulled his own weight on the docks. He'd threatened Eamon before. Eamon'd shrug it off, avoid Honus after hours. But it gnawed at him. He'd go back and fight. But he'd go see Gwen first.

The store was closed, but she'd still do business. He'd paid late visits before, but he was hoping as he walked the rutted dirt street that this one could be different, more personal. It wasn't. She let him in. Took him in the back room and took his last dollar. Tender, passionate. But at a price. And this time Eamon's seed took hold.

It was raining now as he stepped into the street, waving good-bye to Gwen, who'd seen him to the door. Eamon's life had been short on personal connectivity. He'd never been more than a customer. So there was an emptiness in him that evening, a wish that his late-evening visits to Gwen could involve more than just paid-for sex.

No way was he going to fight Honus.

Eamon's room was above The Lion, across the street from the Dyberry Tavern. He circled the long way around, avoiding any confrontation. The night was warm, the rain was light, and Eamon was experiencing something he'd felt more and more often lately. Thoughts beyond work and sleep and eating. As if his brain was starting to expand. Like a self was starting to emerge.

I don't know what thought it was that drove him to climb the cliff. It might have been symbolic: rising above these circumstances, taking a broader view of his life. But soon he was climbing up the muddy hillside that overlooks the town, grasping trees and rocks and hauling himself up toward the top.

It's not a hard climb. The highest point is a couple of hundred feet above town. It's steep, but only the last thirty feet or so are sheer. Even that part is fairly easy to navigate in proper light. But in the dark, with wet, slippery footholds and with several ounces of whiskey slowing one's reactions—that's when it can be hazardous. I have always felt a sickening unease when I've been up there.

Driven by longing, by a simmering rage borne of cowardice, Eamon took one chance too many. As he stretched for a rock that was beyond his grasp, the gravelly shale beneath his feet gave way and he fell, twenty-five feet straight down, cracking his head on a boulder and rolling a distance before coming to rest in a hollow beneath a pine tree.

He never quite regained consciousness. They found him two days later, and he sure looked dead. No one stepped forward to claim the body. There was no one really to miss him.

Chapter Two

This side of the cemetery, away from the big old monuments and the plots from the 1800s and the simple gray stones of farming families. Past the German section, with *Hier ruht in Gott* inscribed in faint script; across the creek, where the slope becomes steeper and that line of hemlocks makes evening as dark as midnight. This is where they buried the indigent—the transient dock workers killed in fights outside bars, the runaways, the prostitutes. No funeral service. No markers. Just dug a hole and threw 'em in with the rocks.

Here. Right at this hook in the path. This is where Herbie had his first encounter.

A couple of years ago Herbie was a wise-ass, cigarette-smoking, smacked-around-by-his-father sophomore in high school who hung out on Main Street every night and, quite incongruously, was a pretty good goalie on the soccer team.

Last year the soccer coach abruptly resigned to take a vice principal's job at a school down near Allentown. The new coach is a total dick of a gym teacher, and Herbie made it very clear he wasn't about to play any more soccer with that guy running the show. The gym teacher took Herbie aside and offered a bit of encouraging guidance.

"Listen, you little shit," he said. "I don't give a rat's ass if you play soccer or not. You can go out for cheerleading for all I care. I'd suggest football or cross-country, but you'd wimp out the first day." Then he made Herbie run laps for the rest of the gym period.

Herbie quit smoking a long time ago, by the way. And to prove the soccer coach wrong, he decided to go out for football and cross-country at the same time.

Herbie wasn't drunk that summer night in the cemetery. They'd taken a six-pack of Rolling Rock out of a spare refrigerator in a guy's father's garage after their Sunday-afternoon shift at the diner, set it against a rock in the river to keep it cold, and drunk two cans apiece. Enough to relax; not enough to stop Herbie from running the mile and a half home when the beer was gone and a few cracks of lightning stopped the party.

It was a cool night for early August, mid-fifties anyway. A good night for running, and Herbie was wearing his Nikes. The moon was nearly full and the quickly moving clouds were thin, so there was enough light, even in the cemetery. It wasn't too late, just after eleven, when he turned off North Main Street and jogged through the cemetery gate, his feet making *shift-shift* sounds on the cindery path.

What'd they been talking about? Their fathers. That always came up. You run along the river here; it never flows hard except after a huge rain or a snowmelt. Tonight it just slides along, big pools, a bit of motion sparkling in the moonlight where the river curves and drops. Lots of big trees overhead; the water's only twenty feet wide here.

The path curves left and you're deeper into the place, the hill behind you cutting off the view from the street. The path gets wider, then narrow as you cross over the creek and into the older section, heading directly toward the cliff.

There's a spring that seeps from the ground partway up that hill, and it trickles over rocks and around stumps after it rains. Lots of the time in summer it doesn't even flow, but the upper path is always damp for a few feet where it passes, and the grass is always lusher right there. Sometimes there's enough water to carry dried hemlock needles, and there are spots where maple leaves bunch up against tree stumps. But even then it's barely a trickle. The water disappears below ground for a few feet beneath the upper path, then emerges at the base of a rock wall and makes a hard turn as the hill becomes steeper. And then it's gone.

What you have there, in a tree-shielded, steep, hard-clay pocket at the farthest edge of the cemetery, is a tiny soupy area, an amalgamation of water from that spring with the energy it's gathered as it trickled over leaves and grass and bear urine and rabbit shit, pooled with the dusty remnants of marrow and tendon, Eamon's memory and fear and confusion. His not-quite death. And lots and lots of time.

Eamon still exists there, and a century plus of on-and-off trickling have eroded much of his unmarked grave site. Tonight a great storm was approaching; the crackling of lightning and the swiftly arriving cold air and even the light from the moon all contributed, caused a cloud in that pocket, a stirring, an energy.

Herbie was running hard now as the rain began in earnest. Carrying his own sort of energy. An energy Eamon could latch onto.

Chapter Three

Eamon's final thoughts as he reached for that rock had held a rare clarity, a self-awareness he'd been lacking. He saw himself for what he was—a coward, but not so far gone that he couldn't overcome it. Just a few steps, an effort to be stronger, to allow himself to grow. Just a small stretch.

And then he was falling, grasping for something, anything, but all there was was air. Dark, wet air and a wind picking up and a couple of flashes of lightning. It took just a second, but in that final second his fear and his anger and his bottled-up passion coalesced and ignited into one hot emotion. And his head hit hard and his teeth mashed his tongue, and bones broke and organs hemorrhaged and blood trickled out of his mouth.

The body didn't die right then. The external bleeding didn't last, but the internal bleeding did, and the body was on the border of life and death when they found him two days later.

There were vague sensations in Eamon of the tastes of blood and dirt, of the smothering mud as they filled his grave, of the chill and the damp and the overall extinguishing. And what was left was pure and eternal but weak. A damaged soul lacking full consciousness; short of the thought and the power to step into a better realm, to follow the light into the afterlife. Just strong enough to stay with the buried body, to cling to what was left. Because the soul resides throughout the body, not just in the heart or in the brain's electrical synapses, but extending through the muscles and bones and fingernails. And the body supports and nourishes the soul, gives it the advantage of physical life until the soul is ready to let go and move on. Most souls know when the time has come. But Eamon was nowhere near ready, and so the opportunity was missed.

More than a century later, Herbie, in the best shape of his life, is running home from the river. Rain in his face, but not too hard, and the sky lighting up with flashes.

"I've never been freaked out or anything in the cemetery," he told a friend at work the next day. "I like running in there, even at night. So I'm about halfway

through, and I'm running sort of fast because I'm getting wet, but I don't want to go too hard because football starts the next morning.

"And then I'm like, 'Who the hell is following me?'
And I look back and there's nobody there, so I run a
little farther and then I stop and turn around and say,
'Who's that?' And there's nobody there, and then there's
this lightning flash, and some of the light just stays
there about six feet from me, and then it gets kind of
wispy and starts to fade. And I'm like, 'Whoa, holy
shit,' and it's moving toward me. So I start laughing
and I start running, and I swear to God the thing keeps
following me. And I'm laughing, but I start sprinting
my ass off to get out of there, and it keeps coming after
me. And by the time I get out of the cemetery, I'm not
laughing anymore and I'm liable to piss in my pants."

Chapter Four

The coaches don't really like this idea, but they're willing to humor Herbie for now. The state says a kid can play two sports in the same season, but limits the amount of practice time he can put in and sets a maximum of three games or competitions per week. The school administration just wishes the kid would go back to soccer—he made first team all-league last fall—but Herbie says, "There's no frickin' way."

So they issue him pads and tell him if he survives two-a-days with the football team this week, he'll be excused early from afternoon sessions next week so he can run with the cross-country team in the evenings. Once school starts he could do some sort of alternating, but he'll never get good at anything if he doesn't make a choice by then. Maybe he'll be a decent placekicker, with that soccer experience.

"I wanna run kicks *back,*" he says. "Yeah, I'll kick

off, too, if they want, but I want to run with the ball. How hard can that be?"

Herbie's very wiry. He does thirty-eight pull-ups at the start of practice. Nobody else does more than thirty, but pull-ups have little to do with football ability.

"He's an athlete, there's no doubt about that," says special-teams coach Lee Conover, who taught Herbie in a class called Introductory Philosophy last spring. "He's a total maverick, though, and that never quite works in a sport like this. Kickoffs and punt team, he could be an asset. I could see him on the cross-country team, but two sports at once? Come on."

They run some passing drills, mostly simple square-outs, and Herbie can certainly catch the ball. Can he hold on to it when he gets hit? They'll find out in a hurry. One of the coaches calls all of the backs and receivers to the side of the field. "Nutcrackers," he says.

This is a drill in which two players lie helmet to helmet on their backs. At the whistle, the coach tosses the football at them. Whoever gets to it first tries to pick it up and run. The other guy has to bring him down. Almost anything goes.

Herbie gets down with Lenny Johnson, who'll prob-ably start at tailback this fall. The whistle blows. Ball hits Herbie squarely in the side of the helmet and bounces away. Johnson grabs it, Herbie leaps for his ankle and misses, and Johnson trots away as Herbie tries to scramble to his feet.

"Always have to be ready for the ball, Herbie," the coach says. "Try it again."

This time he's with Eric Diaz, a junior linebacker. Whistle blows, they both jump up, and the ball lands between them, rolling around. Herbie gets there first, but all he can do is smother the ball while Diaz comes down on top of him hard.

"Better," Coach says. "Priority one is getting the football."

He gets back in line. He runs the drill six more times and gets the ball twice. The only time he actually gets to his feet, he gets drilled to the ground in a second. On defense he looks really bad a couple of times but makes a few decent tackles, too.

All right, it won't be easy, he thinks as they run laps after practice. *But it'll be okay. I'll figure this out.*

Chapter Five

Here's a little story about Herbie. Back in kindergarten they're putting on this end-of-the-year concert for parents and siblings. They're up on the stage in the auditorium, and the finale is this cowboy type of song where everybody claps together in rhythm at certain points. I notice that Herbie, looking kind of smug in the second row, is clapping a half beat later than everyone else. It's not that he can't keep up; he's obviously doing it on purpose.

After the show he comes up to me. "Hey, Frank," he says, "did you notice that I was the only one clapping in unison?"

"Yeah," I said. "I definitely noticed."

He nods and gives a wicked grin. "The teacher thought I was the only one doing it *wrong.*"

———

"You know I'm goin' back tonight," Herbie told Kevin while they were washing dishes at work this evening. "I mean, it scared the piss out of me, but it was still cool," he says. "I never seen a ghost before. Never even thought about them." I don't think Herbie quite believes that he actually saw a ghost. He's not showing enough fear.

"This was like, I don't know, a force or something. Like it was clawing at me. I wasn't feeling anything that hurt, but it was definitely making contact, and I think if I'd been running any slower it would have had me. It felt like dust being hurled at me, but as if it was intact, not floating apart like a handful of dust would. Staying together but slipping off me.

"So, yeah, I'm going back. What can it do? Kill me?"

Herbie goes back and forth from our mom's house to our dad's but spends most of his time at our mom's. It was an ice-cold dynamic when the four of us were under one roof, with Dad always pissed off about his job and taking it out on his wife and me and Herbie. Mostly just being sour and yelling once in a while, but using a slap or a fist when he thought that he needed to. It began to fall apart when Herbie was eight, and I was seventeen and developed lymphatic cancer and died. Totally crushed my dad's spirit.

By the time he was in seventh grade, Herbie was avoiding home life by spending every evening hanging out in front of the Turkey Hill convenience store with whatever crowd showed up. Before he'd leave for the evening, he'd put a Dylan CD on repeat in his room for me, since that was who I'd been listening to constantly in the months before I died. He always whispered, "See ya, Frank," as he left the room. Herbie never once said good-bye to Dad as he slipped out the side door, though.

Tensions in the house eased a bit when Dad moved out a year or so ago and Herbie started working part-time at the diner.

Most of his friends think of Herbie as a bit of a wise guy who won't go very far in life. He never told anybody how exceptionally high his SAT scores are or that his grade-point average ranks fourth in the class. That he wants to study quantum physics in college. Most people don't know any of that, just like they don't recognize what great physical condition he's in. They think of him as a guy who smokes and hangs out on Main Street. They're a couple of years behind in their thinking.

Tonight there's a strong breeze and the sky is clear as Herbie walks along River Road in the dark toward the cemetery, approaching from the opposite end, passing through the gates at the point that he left the place last night.

He's alone; it's after eleven. He's got a flashlight in his pocket, but there's enough moonlight that he doesn't need it yet. Maybe when he gets deeper into the place and back under the thick evergreens. For now he can see just fine.

Herbie has only visited my grave a couple of times since I died, just looking at the gravestone from several feet away before walking on. I think he knows I'm not there. Instead, he talks to me in the woods behind the school, taking walks back there once in a while in the early evening before dark. He speaks out loud to me. I can tell that he has doubts about whether I'm there, but he keeps talking just in case I am.

I am. Although I'm not always "conscious" in this afterlife state, it is easy for Herbie to make me aware. When I hear him speaking to me, I'm always able to get to him. But I do have gaps in which I don't realize that a good deal of time has passed. The mind is mysterious. I don't always know where I've been.

Herbie is looking around at the gravestones and the trees. Alert. Stepping carefully and slowly, walking with his shoulders back, his fingers spread slightly, his mouth half open. He's aware of the sound of every footstep he takes, crushing the soft grass.

A shape on the hillside, moving slowly. He clicks
on the flashlight and catches green eyes shining back—
a deer. It freezes in the light. Herbie clicks it off. The
deer stares for a moment, then takes a few quick strides
away. Herbie exhales. Keeps walking.

The thing was following him tightly through here
last night, latched on and frantic. That feeling had come
back to Herbie in his dreams, the feeling of something
wanting to grasp him, almost to ride him like a jockey.
The feeling of his arm hairs standing on end and his
eyes open wide and his mouth stuck fast in a gape. But
more than anything, he remembered that feeling of
speed as he sprinted his ass out of there. God, he ran
fast. Driven by fear and exhilaration. Some combination
of those two emotions. Like ice water in his veins. I
know that feeling; I miss it badly.

Around a bend in the path; some huge old tombstones in this section. Low railings marking family
plots, smaller stones surrounding massive rectangular
monuments with names like Barrable, Penniman, and
Torrey—wealthy families from the middle of the nine-
teenth century. The trees are much thicker here, tower-
ing pines that were seedlings when Eamon Connelly
was buried. Herbie senses something now, maybe just
the seclusion of the place, the mystery.

He keeps going forward, measuring his steps on the grassy path. He's deep into the cemetery, midway through and near the steepest hillside. His foot slips where the path becomes murky, and this is the spot, the place where he first became aware last night that he was not alone.

He stops and looks around, his eyes adjusting to the deeper darkness. All is still around him. He hears nothing unusual, a gentle motion in the treetops; the breeze on his arms. But he is aware. He is six hundred yards from either gate. He swallows hard and gives a half-hearted laugh at himself, not sure whether it's for putting himself in this position or for believing that there might be some risk.

"There ain't no such thing as ghosts," he mutters, so softly that a person standing next to him wouldn't have heard it. But Herbie hears it, and the sound of his own *stssss* trailing off with the word *ghosts* gives him pause. *Sure there is,* he's thinking now. *They're all around me.*

He straightens up a bit, raises his chin to look farther above him, into the branches, where he can see bits of sky and thin misty clouds illuminated by the moon. He could go, he could run. And if he did, would he be followed? Would that thing or others like it come jetting toward his head? Are they waiting now for him to move? He takes a step forward, then another. Puts his fingertips to his face, his palms resting tight against his chin. Smells his own warmth. Dares to speak in a whisper.

"Hey."

He is quiet for a long moment. There is no reply, no motion. But his voice has set himself at ease; perhaps it has done the same for another. "It's cool," he says, trying to sound calm. "I'm harmless."

And the sensation is not sudden this time. He is barely aware that he has been engulfed by a thin dampness, cooler than sweat, and with purpose. He brushes his arm, and the stuff feels like wet powder, slippery and gelatinous but with almost no thickness at all. A flick of his hand makes it swirl like a fog, but it doesn't dissipate.

"What the hell is this?" Herbie says quietly. "Who are you?"

It swirls up and above him now, circling ever so slowly, not quite taking form but not scattering either. Herbie turns his head to follow it, and it settles toward the earth a few yards away, standing as tall as a man and as wide.

Herbie stares, barely breathing. He sees no features,

nothing like a head or a torso. But the thing has a presence, an undeniable consciousness. Herbie has been touched and internalized. He takes a step backward and waits. Takes another step back. And another. One careful step at a time until he is forty yards away. The thing has not followed him this time. Herbie moves faster, and now he is running. He is running faster than he's ever run in his life.

Chapter Six

Herbie logs on to the Internet when he gets home and posts this message in the physics chat room he frequents:

goalie *8/12 23:57* Here is a theory. It's weird shit, but just join me in the cemetery some night if you want to see weirder. All around us are these specks: tiny, less-than-microscopic universes where the sense of time and distance is just like it is for us, but on a much smaller scale. A being on a planet in that universe would live its entire lifetime in what for us would be a fraction of a second, but from their perspective it lasts seventy or a hundred years. And this little dot of a universe they live in seems infinite to them. The distance from one end of their universe to the other

seems just as vast as ours; it has billions of
galaxies like ours does; thousands of popula-
tions of intelligent life living light-years
apart and wondering if there's anyone else out
there. Trillions of these little universes
could fit into your hand, and you wouldn't
even know they were there. And at the same
time, our own universe is nothing but a speck
in some vastly larger universe, and what we
think of as infinite time and unending space is
too small to even be perceptible to whatever
lives there. So our entire existence, not just
our lifetimes but even the 14 billion years
since the big bang, is a blink of the eye in
the perspective of the larger universe. And
that giant universe is a speck within an even
bigger one, and on and on in both directions.
In the time it took me to write this, billions
of years have passed in the smaller universes.
But it would take billions of years of our time
to equal a few seconds on the next level up.
Everything is relative. Everything we think
about time and distance are a result of the
scale of the universe we live in. In the mean-
time, this is where we're at. Nobody knows why
we're here; if it just happened by accident or

if some intelligent thing invented it. And nobody knows what comes next.

My brother Frank visits me sometimes in my dreams. Most of my dreams are very chaotic, and I remember very few of them. But every few months, I have a calm and vivid dream, and I enter a room and my brother is there and he says that everything is good, that he's okay and he's happy and he still exists. It's not the same dream every time but seems like a new visit, an update. I never think to ask during the dream where he is or who he is with. But in the most recent dream, last weekend, he said, "Herbie, life is what you make it." And most of me says this is just my subconscious at work, bullshitting me that there's an after-life and that the people I love who died are there together, and they're still happy and caring and intelligent. And a growing part of me thinks it really is true, that conscious-ness goes on even after the body expires.

Chapter Seven

"Nice one," Coach says as Herbie lofts a high, spiraling punt that bounces at the five-yard line and trickles out of bounds. "If you can punt like that under pressure, you'll be great."

"What about the other end of it?" Herbie asks. "Can I try running some back?"

"Yeah, what the hell," Coach says. "Get down there. Eric! Come in here and kick a few. We'll see what Herbie can do on returns."

Herbie trots over to the other end of the field and sets up at about the fifteen. This is the sixth practice in three days, and he's got bruised ribs and a swollen wrist, but he can run.

The ball is coming toward him now, end over end. He trots a couple of steps forward and sidesteps to his left, getting under the ball and catching it against his chest. Already the defenders are approaching, six yards away and going full tilt. Herbie steps right, then pivots and takes off toward the left sideline, eluding the first two and picking up a block that sets him into the clear. It's a race along the sideline now. Herbie tucks the ball into his left arm and cuts up the field. Two guys pin him in and he hesitates, cutting sharply back toward the center of the field, where he's met with a hard tackle and the ball pops loose. Bodies scramble on top of the ball. The coach blows his whistle.

"Pretty good return, but you have to hold on to the ball. No excuses. No fumbles. Try it again."

He runs back six more, doesn't fumble again, and nearly breaks one all the way before the punter runs him down. Practice ends with that play; they tack these special-teams drills on at the very end. Now it's five laps around the field and showers.

"Herbie," Coach Conover says to him as he's walking off the field. He tosses him a football. "A little present. You carry this ball everywhere you go for the next couple of days. Make it a part of yourself. Sleep with it. Learn not to fumble. You can be a decent return man if you can hang on to the ball. Otherwise, forget it. Fumbled punts kill ball games."

"Got ya," Herbie says. He holds the ball at arm's length and squints at it. "Guess I'll have to get rid of my teddy bear to make room for it in bed."

Chapter Eight

Let me state right here that I cannot directly interfere with what goes on in my brother Herbie's life. I do not have the inclination (or the *ability*) to appear as a ghost, because my spirit is no longer connected to anything physical; there is nothing tangible that I can conjure up in the way that Eamon Connelly apparently can. Eamon can do it because some fraction of his worldly self is still intact, however fragile. Just enough that he can somehow latch onto Herbie's energy and re-exist. He needs Herbie's spirit, his life force, to propel him. I do not know why Eamon can connect with my brother. I can't contact Eamon. We exist on different planes.

I made a clean break from my body when I died, like nearly everyone does. Yes, I can still witness what goes on on Earth, and I still care. I can come and go from your realm as I wish, but I cannot influence what occurs there. Herbie's reference to my appearance in his dreams is not entirely wishful thinking on his part, but it is only in his dream state that he can be open to my approach. He's a cynical little bastard. My first few "appearances" in his dreams were met with immediate waking and cold sweats and many subsequent nights of insomnia. Gradually he came to view these occasional visits as subconscious fabrications of his vivid imagination. Now he sort of half-believes that they're real.

The dream visits *are* real, but they are not much different from any of my other visits. He says that I speak to him, but that is not yet true. The words he has "heard" have come from himself. I have not figured out how to communicate directly. It is apparent to me that when he is dreaming, I can slip into his subconscious; he can see me. I do not know how to take that further, to bridge the gap and converse.

There is so much that I left undone when I died. So many things on Earth that I still want to do, many of them admirable and many of them selfish. Things I never got to do when I had a body, particularly things I could have done in tandem with other bodies. That need hasn't ever left me. It hasn't ever been relieved.

I have eons of learning ahead of me. If you want to know the truth, I don't know jackshit about the afterlife. I have only been dead for ten years.

Chapter Nine

Herbie jogs along Main Street, a couple of minutes late for work. They'll understand; it's either arrive late or do without a shower after a two-hour football workout in mid-August heat.

He enters the kitchen through the back door. Tony is at the sink scrubbing a pot that the chef made turkey soup in. Kevin is chopping iceberg lettuce for the salad bar.

"Who you gonna call?" Tony says, grinning, repeating the line from *Ghostbusters*. Herbie had filled these guys in on the cemetery encounters.

"It's Peter Venkman!" Kevin adds. Neither of these guys is particularly clever. They used both of those jokes yesterday.

Herbie joins Kevin at the table and starts opening a giant can of chickpeas. "You check the dressings?" he asks.

"No. I just got here, too," Kevin says. "I figured I better get the main stuff out there or Jackson would throw a fit."

Herbie is unofficially in charge of these other two high-school kids. All three started working at the diner within a couple of weeks of one another last year, but Kevin and Tony don't have much common sense. So Herbie is always given the assignments by Jackson, the manager, and decides who should do what as far as food preparation and cleanup.

He steps out the swinging doors into the dining room. The salad bar looks crappy—slivers of cheese in the olive tray, French dressing dripped across the counter, watery-looking cucumber slices. He grabs a wipe and cleans up most of the spillage in a hurry, then takes several of the containers back to the kitchen to refill them.

"So, did you figure out who this is that's chasing you?" Kevin asks with a smirk.

Herbie shakes his head. "Nah. Some dead psycho." He laughs. "Wants to possess me." He flexes his skinny biceps and goes into a bodybuilder pose. "Who wouldn't, you know?"

Kevin whacks a tomato with the knife. "Scary shit, man," but he's grinning.

"I'll kick his ass if I have to," Herbie says. "I mean, me versus dead plasma. You have to give me the edge, don't you think?"

"I don't know, man," Kevin says. "You won't catch me out there alone."

"I wouldn't worry if I was you," Herbie says with a smirk. "I feel like I've been singled out to be haunted. The chosen one. I don't think you'd get hassled."

"You better be careful." Kevin points the knife at Herbie and looks at him hard. "I ain't shittin' ya. I wouldn't go looking for trouble if I was you."

Herbie laughs it off. He can't think of any clever line, though. "I ain't scared," he says.

"My grandmother says spooky shit goes on in that cemetery. People who got murdered like a hundred years ago walking around in there." Kevin glances over at Tony, who's up to his elbows in the sink, scrubbing more pots. He lowers his voice. "She said one night when she was a kid she took a shortcut through there just after dark—it was Halloween—and some crazy guy bleeding came running at her swinging a shovel. She swung her trick-or-treat bag at him, and it went right through him, and he started laughing and just floated away and dissolved."

"Really?"

"I swear to God. She wouldn't say it if it wasn't true. She's like a frickin' hard-core Catholic. You should go talk to her, man. She's heard every story there is."

Herbie just nods, stares ahead for a few seconds. "I'm gonna check the storeroom," he says. "We're getting low on olives."

Herbie was unusually quiet for the rest of the shift, and declined to hang out with Kevin and Tony after. He headed for our father's house instead, a tiny, drafty two-bedroom rental by the river on Court Street. Dad was awake, watching a Yankees game in his underwear and drinking a bottle of Yuengling beer.

"What's up, Idjit?" Dad said as Herbie opened the front door.

"Not much, Dad. What's going on?"

"Bottom of the ninth. They're down a run. You want a beer?"

"Shit-yeah. I'll get it." He steps into the kitchen. Dishes are piled in the sink; a greasy frying pan on the stove top; empty bottles and cans lined up along the counters. "You only got one left," Herbie calls as he opens the refrigerator.

"That's all right. Go ahead. I'll pick up more tomorrow. Shit—he struck him out!"

"That game?"

"Two outs."

Herbie twists off the beer cap and sits down. "I'm frickin' beat, man. Two sessions tomorrow, then a scrimmage on Saturday. Monday I start cross-country."

Dad shakes his head and laughs. "You're an animal."

"Yeah. I almost broke one today. Fielded a punt and ran it wide. Coach says I might play some wingback. And I'm on all the special teams—kicking and receiving."

"Not bad for a skinny twerp."

Used to be if Dad called Herbie that, he'd mean it as an insult, but things have lightened up considerably. I don't think the guy was ever cut out to be a family man. Having to live with rules like vacuuming and cleaning toilets is totally foreign to him. So was trying to nurture his kids. So if he can live like a slob and hang out with Herbie like this, he's happy, more or less. We come from a long line of seedy relatives.

"You believe in ghosts, Dad?"

"What?"

"Ghosts."

"I don't believe in anything. You die, you're dead. It's cruel but true, buddy. The only ghosts are in people's heads."

Herbie nods and doesn't push it. No sense taking this further. Neither of our parents have ever discussed death—especially mine—with Herbie.

The game ends a few minutes later, and they switch to a sitcom rerun. Herbie falls asleep in the armchair, his beer barely touched, and Dad falls asleep on the couch. They stay like that until well after midnight, when Herbie wakes up to take a piss. He nudges Dad, and they go upstairs to the bedrooms.

Dad has photos of Herbie and me on his dresser. He says good night to us both every evening. Sometimes he fills me in on things—how the Yankees did; Herbie got his hair cut; saw your mom this morning, and she looked like she's doing well; "Miss ya, kiddo."

I know it.

A morning-long intrasquad scrimmage on Saturday in intense heat and humidity. Guys are coming off the field and just laying flat on the grass, pouring cups of water through their face masks. It's hot.

Herbie hasn't gotten in yet, but it's early. He's kneeling on the sideline, trading friendly insults with his friend Gordon Shuler, the second-string quarterback. Gordon throws a nice ball but tends to trip over his own feet. He's tall and gawky.

"Herbie," Gordon says. "What are you gonna do when you're carrying the ball and you see Phil coming straight toward you, ready to knock you on your ass and step all over you?"

Phil Weiss is a 280-pound defensive tackle.

"Jump, I guess. Give me a break. He's slow as shit. One move and I'm past him."

"What if Purvis is coming from the other direction?"

"Hey, I'm the punter, right? I'll just kick it in a hurry and say I forgot what play it was supposed to be."

"Yeah, right."

"Or I'll just lateral it back to you. Let you deal with it."

"Thanks."

"Anyway, by the time I get in there, those guys will have sweated off about fifty pounds, so it'll be a little more even."

"Yeah. And maybe Casper the Friendly Ghost will throw a block or two for you."

Herbie smirks and turns his head sideways to face Gordon. "Who you been talking to?"

"Went to a séance."

"Get out."

"Kevin told me."

"That greasy bastard."

A call comes from down the sideline. "Herbie! Get in there and punt."

Herbie jumps up and fastens his chin strap and trots onto the field. The offense is across midfield, so he has a chance to really pin one down near the end zone. He wipes his hands on his knees and exhales in a steady stream. He's punted under pressure before, but this is close to the real thing. The defense will be bearing down on him in a hurry.

He calls signals and the ball is snapped, a bit high and fading to the left. Herbie has to leap to snare it and comes down off balance. Phil Weiss has broken through and is coming toward him, but Herbie gets the kick away before being flattened by the big guy.

Herbie starts to get up, but Weiss keeps him pinned down. He rolls and escapes and gets to his feet, and already Lenny Johnson has crossed the forty on the return and is a step ahead of his pursuers. Herbie accelerates and chases him toward the sideline, gaining an inch for every yard he runs. He has a good angle and gets close enough to finally leap at the ten, wrapping his arms around Lenny's legs and dragging him down near the goal line.

"Great return!" the coach is yelling. "And good pursuit, Herbie. You other guys on the punt team, where the heck were you? That coverage was piss poor, boys. We gotta do better than that."

Herbie catches his breath and jogs off the field. He made an impact. That counts for something.

"Olympic sprinter," Shuler remarks as Herbie joins him on the sideline. He holds out a hand for Herbie to slap. "I ain't kidding. You're fast as hell."

"Yeah. I can move."

"Some supernatural aid out there?"

"Nah." Herbie laughs. "That was all me that time, brother."

Chapter Ten

Herbie checks the Internet physics board to see if there are any replies to his recent manifesto about his multi-universe theory and the afterlife. A few of the regulars have responded.

cosmo-not *8/13 23:13* First, forget the brotherly ghost stuff. No way, no how. (Okay, MAYBE! but I'd have to see this haunter with my own two eyes.) Prove it or move it--hit one of the paranormal boards if you want to ramble on about that sh*t.

rsingh *8/14 19:19* Life has many, many layers my friend, and most are not physical. Of course your brother still exists. Continue to seek him.

chipper *8/14 20:27* So no big bang, Goalie, just a zillion little bubbles? I cud see that. Ded brother, huh? That sux.

Herbie responds:

goalie *8/15 16:42* Yes it sucks that my brother died. Seventeen years old! That's how old I am. This is the best time of my life, or at least it will be. Frank would have pitched for the varsity if he hadn't died. He'd probably be married by now with kids of his own. He would have laughed a billion times.

———

The difference between Herbie and me—between you and me—is much smaller than you think. The difference is almost literally transparent; I am transparent, and you have physical substance. But my journey toward the afterlife's innermost circle—that realm where guys like Jesus and Muhammad and George Harrison are said to hang out—is only a fraction of a step farther along than any of you on Earth are. I am far closer to you than I am to them. I also know that I haven't made much effort to get closer. I figure it will take most of eternity to get there anyway, so why hurry? I'm still a lot more interested in how Herbie's football team will do against Pocono than I am in eternal enlightenment.

I cannot see the future; very few of us can. (It hasn't *happened* yet!) But I can, with some difficulty, review the past. My ability to do that is limited and superficial. Time moves in circles, and though it does not repeat itself, there are vantage points from which we can see past events as if they are presently unfolding, in what I can describe as something like parallel universes, or layers of time and energy. For example, I have witnessed the events I described earlier concerning Eamon Connelly's final day of "life." I can view his past quite clearly and with a great deal of depth, and I think I can do so because Eamon is easy to find. He has remained stuck in that time, in that place, on that layer of existence. I discovered him because I was following my brother, and because Eamon and Herbie crossed paths. I can watch his life (and death) almost as if it were my own.

When I was alive, I had frequent feelings of having been in places before, even though I knew for certain that I hadn't. That I'd already visited the cellar of a building that I was just stepping into for the first time in my life, for example, or that a thought I had while sitting on a bench in the park in front of the courthouse had passed through my head in some much earlier time. Déjà vu, they call it. I had it regularly.

Our grandfather died about three years ago, and I was here to greet him when he came over. He did not know me, just as he hadn't really known anyone on Earth when he died. The effects of Alzheimer's had destroyed his memory, and the memory, after all, is what makes us human. But those effects are reversible in the afterlife, and gradually Grandpa has begun to become more whole. In time he will be himself again.

Many who die have a long line of relatives and friends waiting here for them, but I had been alone until Grandpa arrived. Maybe that's why I've remained so tied to earthly observations and have resisted most things ethereal. I have spent nearly all my time here either reviewing events of my own physical life, checking in on others who are still alive, or watching after Herbie. I went to my own funeral, have spent many, many hours in my old bedroom. I admit to a feeling of being cheated out of my best physical years, and yes, I have sometimes been very lonely. And very much afraid.

Others float around up here in states of apparent bliss. Well, why wouldn't they? They've shed their bodies, they don't need them. They used their bodies up—they built houses and ran marathons and spawned children and fished for marlin. Sure they can work toward inner peace and nirvana. They aren't cursed with eternal virginity like I am.

Chapter Eleven

"Twice now," Herbie says. He and Kevin are sitting in Kevin's grandmother's kitchen on East Street. It's late Monday afternoon. Out the window you can look across the Dyberry Creek and see the edge of the cemetery. Herbie is looking that way. "I haven't gone back for a few nights."

"Well, even if it's frightening, you should probably go back soon," she says. "There are only certain times when a spirit like that is active. It can be decades before it gets stirred up again. I've heard stories of ghosts who were quite active for a time, then were never seen again for fifty years or more. Suddenly they were back, with no clues to where they'd been for all that time, or why they ever returned."

Kevin's grandmother—they call her Winnie—has lived her entire life on this block. She's a tiny, white-haired woman, hands knobby with arthritis. The cemetery was her playground as a girl. Her late husband proposed to her on a walk in there. She pushed her baby strollers through there almost every day, and for years has gathered pinecones there for Christmas decorations. She knows the place as well as anybody.

"Whoever this is, he's active this summer, and you seem to be part of the reason," she says. "Most of these ghosts, they appear only to certain individuals. Your family has been here a long time?"

"Yeah," Herbie says. "Way back. My mother's side since the twenties. My father's side since the turn of the century at least. My grandfather died a couple of years ago. He was born here. Both his parents, too. I don't know any earlier than that. It's sketchy."

"And many of them are buried over there?" she asks, nodding toward the cemetery.

"Pretty much all of them."

Kevin butts in. "His brother died when we were little," he says.

"That ain't my brother," Herbie says sharply.

"How do you know?"

"No friggin' way," Herbie says. "I'd know Frank. Believe me." He gives Kevin a glare.

Kevin shrugs. "Okay."

Winnie smiles at Herbie. "There's a storm coming tonight. Why don't you walk through there?" She glances at Kevin. "*Alone.* Walk through the next several nights and see what happens. Whoever this is, he wants something from you. There may be some way you can help him. That may be all that he needs."

Herbie rubs his chin. He had a bad case of acne a couple of years back, but it's mostly clear now, just a few hard little bumps and some whiskers. "Okay," he says after a minute. "I gotta get to cross-country practice. But why me? This thing is all over me when I go in there."

Winnie gives him a long look. "You've got something." She raises her hand slowly and waves it across in front of him. "A nice safe aura. Like a peacemaker."

Kevin lets out a laugh. "No way. He gets in fights like once a month at least."

Herbie gives him a little shove. "I don't." He looks at Winnie. "I never start nothing. But I'll take a guy out if he messes with me."

"Well," she says, "there's amazing energy in that cemetery. It's scary, but it's beautiful. There are a lot of restless souls around. One of them has latched onto you."

Cross-country practice doesn't start until six-thirty to avoid the afternoon heat. They gather up at the track. It's a big group; boys' and girls' teams under the same coach.

"At the beginning of the summer I sent you each a letter outlining what you should do to prepare for the season," the coach says. "All of you follow it?"

Most of the kids nod and say yeah. Herbie puts up his hand. "I never got the letter."

"Been running anyway?"

"Yeah. I'm in shape."

"We'll see. The rest of you know that we start every season with a two-mile time trial on the track. If you're not ready, it'll be pretty obvious.

"Ron, stretch 'em out and jog a mile or so on the grass," Coach says to the captain. "We'll run it in two sections, boys then girls."

Herbie didn't expect a race the first night, but he can handle it. He does a quick count of about thirty guys out for the team. A lot of them are wrestlers and basketball players just running to stay in shape, but there's a hard-core group of distance runners and other track guys. The team is loaded. The captain, Ron, won the district title as a junior and is a potential all-stater this fall.

Ron goes straight to the lead when the coach blows the whistle, and only two other guys go with him. Herbie sits in the middle of the pack for a couple of laps, feeling relaxed enough. By the mile, the first three are well ahead, and Herbie is still in the trailing pack of about ten as they pass in 5:21. He's run a 5:18 in the physical-fitness test they have to do every spring in gym class, but he still has another mile to go.

He's starting to suck wind a bit, but most of the others are struggling, too. Three others have broken away from the second pack by the time they've finished five laps, and Herbie is now sitting tenth with another six or seven runners on his heels.

"Relax and work," the coach says. "Suck it up. Races are farther than this, boys. This is easy."

It's not easy, and Herbie is feeling it in his shoulders and his sides. He's working to stay in this pack; you lose contact and you fall off the map.

After seven laps, Herbie is with two other guys, about twenty yards behind the eighth-place runner. Ron is sprinting up the track behind them, finishing the race after lapping half the field. Herbie is groaning with every step. He feels like he's sprinting, but he isn't.

The three of them stay clumped together, laboring and really slowing down. On the final turn the short guy with red hair takes off, and Herbie tries to give chase, but he's got nothing left for a kick. He finishes tenth in 11:37, not bad at all for a first effort.

"Walk, guys!" the coach hollers after them. "Walk and get some water in you. Nice job."

The last thing Herbie wants is water; it'd come right

back up. He walks a slow lap by himself, taking off his T-shirt and wiping his forehead with it.

Ron comes jogging up to him, circling the track in the opposite direction. "Herbie," he says.

"Ron."

"You showed up."

"Shit-yeah. I'm serious."

"You actually ran pretty good. You might help us."

"I intend to," Herbie says. "I'm in shape. That's just a long way to race. I'll get used to it."

Ron nods and jogs off. Herbie stops and watches him go. *Effortless,* he thinks.

The girls' race is starting, and Herbie moves to an outside lane. He watches the pack of girls swoop by— lean bodies, ponytails bouncing. More than a few he wouldn't mind knowing better. This might be better than football.

Herbie walks stiffly into the house. "Hey, Mom," he says.

"Hi, babe. Hungry?"

"Yeah. I'm starved. And I'm dead. I didn't expect the Olympic championship on the first night."

She laughs. "No one would think any less of you if you dropped one of the sports, you know."

"*I* would," he says. "I can handle it. This was like

some surprise torture test tonight. He says it'll be saner
for the next couple of weeks."

"Well, get to bed early for once."

"Soon as I eat. Whatta we got?"

"I'll fry you a hamburger."

He sits at the kitchen table and rubs his eyes with
his fists. "We got any juice, Ma?"

"I'm sure we do."

"I'm frickin' thirsty. I'm so frickin' thirsty I could
die."

He eats and goes to his room to lie down and is
immediately out cold. He sleeps hard for about four
hours and wakes up at one-thirty, still thirsty but alert.
He looks around the room. His window is open, and
the breeze is blowing through, cooler and damp. He
hears a low rumble of thunder. He switches on the
light, looks around for a sweatshirt, and walks quietly
down the stairs. There's a liter bottle of Coke in the
refrigerator, half empty and flat. He adds about six
ounces of water, shakes it up, and downs it in several
hard swallows. Then he puts on his running shoes and
carefully opens the door to the outside.

He walks half a block and crosses Main, which is
empty. All of the stores are dark except the Turkey Hill
convenience mart, which now stays open twenty-four
hours. There's no one in there except a clerk. Herbie

crosses the river and walks down toward the YMCA, then cuts onto River Road and takes that very dark street toward the cemetery.

There are only a handful of houses here, flush up against the steep wooded grade that leads to the cliff that overlooks the town. He reaches the cemetery gate. He has forgotten his flashlight. The rain has begun— scattered drops blowing diagonally through the trees. The wind is at his back. It is much cooler than daytime.

He steps off the path and circles through the grass around the large plot of the Appley family. He has admired this plot on other occasions, the low circular fence, the marble benches for visits, the small squarish gravestones of the many children who died in the age before antibiotics. He recalls that I at least had seventeen years; many of the kids in this cemetery didn't get seventeen *days.*

He walks slowly, glancing around. It's thunderstorm season, and one is arriving in a hurry. He sees a flash of lightning, then another, and feels a more consistent tapping of cold raindrops on his neck.

He steps even more carefully as he approaches the site of his previous encounters, inhaling, holding, exhaling slowly. His eyebrows are up, his mouth half open and dry.

A close-by crack of thunder and a jagged lightning

Chapter Twelve

The afterlife. For me, I must admit, a lot of it is voyeurism. We're supposed to be pure spirits, with no interest in physical things like competition or sex. It's said to be all about broadening our intelligence, seeking truth and inner peace and all of that. But it's not always true. Eventually you get to that state, or so I hear, but I've shed very few of my physical desires.

I was seventeen when I died, almost exactly the age Herbie is now, and I left with precious little experience in erotic things. And so even though I no longer have any physical components, I'm left with a yearning that can never be satisfied.

As I have said, I am unable to "haunt," in the sense that I would be perceived by anyone alive. It is true that Herbie has reached a place of awareness when I come to him in dreams, but I have not yet discovered how to reappear in any tangible way.

bolt across the sky. He turns his head, looks behind him, then around. The air is wet and charged.

He walks on. The main path, mostly rutted dirt but with sections of gravel, forms a figure eight through the cemetery; two large loops that join in the middle where a flat wooden bridge crosses the creek. Herbie reaches the bridge and stops.

He does a slow full rotation, scanning the trees and the tombstones for anything that might move. He sees nothing, but feels that he is being watched. He scans again and walks on.

This half of the cemetery is flatter and less wooded, and it's where nearly all new burials are done. My grave is not far from where Herbie is walking, but there is nothing left there of my spirit. There are many old grave sites; the oldest date back to the 1840s. The wealthiest families tended heavily toward the other loop, of course.

The rain gets stronger, and Herbie finds himself in the open, moving away from the trees. "Screw this," he says as his wet shirt quickly sticks to his skin. He turns and jogs back toward the bridge.

He loops around, his calves feeling tight from those circuits of the track earlier this evening. But it feels good to run with a hefty breeze after all that work he's been doing in the heat.

He reaches the bridge, looks up, and stops dead in his tracks.

Eamon Connelly, transparent but fully formed, is not ten feet away, staring at Herbie and slowly raising his hand from his side. He is the color of a sepia-toned photograph, a gentle grayish brown. He has the face of a very young man, a tight line of a mouth, no real hint of facial hair or sideburns, a prominent nose, clear eyes studying Herbie in bewilderment.

"Holy shit," Herbie says in a whisper. He leans slightly forward but does not dare move.

Eamon's hand is raised now, just to chest level, and he pulls his fist tightly to his ribs. Eamon is naked; his thin arms and legs seem slightly long for the size of his body, which is lean and no taller than Herbie's. His feet, as well, are somewhat oversized.

They stare at each other. Herbie takes one step back, and Eamon seems to jump in alarm, lifting into the air several inches and floating off to the side. He hovers for a few seconds, then settles back to the bridge. The look on his face is of fear or confusion.

Herbie looks into those eyes. He is not afraid that he will be harmed, but is astonished at what he's discovered. The spirit transcends the body. There's no denying it now.

"Do you know that you're de genuine concern in his voice.

Eamon shows no sign of hearing that Herbie has spoken. But he raises begins to float again, circling above Herb him. There's another flash of lightning, a of thunder. Eamon fades quickly and is gone

Herbie stares at the space. "Jesus Christ," "The son of a bitch looked just like me."

To reconnect in any meaningful way, one must have a physical or emotional link with someone still alive, so I don't understand why Eamon can do it. There must be a connection. I am able to follow Herbie and interact with him slightly because we were extraordinarily close as kids. I was nearly ten years older than him; it was almost like having a son of my own. We'd play ball in the yard and I'd take him to movies, and we'd wrestle in the living room and I'd tell him stories—ghost stories sometimes—at bedtime. He was my little buddy. It hurt so much to see him missing me so terribly when I died. I wanted so badly to let him know I was all right and that we'd be together again one day and I'd be watching over him until then. But I couldn't. It took years for me to find a way to connect at all. It was only when his mind opened up a bit, when he started pondering eternal questions and reading up on quantum physics and parallel universes that he finally became receptive to my dream visits.

Herbie filled a need in me. For as long as I can remember, I felt incomplete in some small way, like a part of me was missing. Herbie's energy and humor and spark filled in a lot of that gap. The gap has grown bigger since I died.

Herbie was asleep, dreaming that he was climbing a stairway toward an apartment above a Main Street store. A party was going on in the apartment—kids from his school drinking beer and listening to music. The door was open and he entered, but instead of turning into the living room where the party was, he stepped into the kitchen and found me leaning against the refrigerator.

"Hi, Frank," he said, as if he was expecting to find me there.

"Hey, buddy."

"Got out of work late," he said. "Big rush toward the end."

"Tough break."

"Yeah. I'm greasy as hell from scrubbing pots."

"You'll live."

"I know." He laughed. "Lot of girls here?"

"Looks that way."

It's easy to fool yourself when you're dreaming. Herbie showed no surprise that we were standing there talking or that we both seemed to be about the same age instead of ten years apart. And I was fooling myself, too, dreaming that I was solid and alive, that I'd really just been waiting for him to get out of work and join me at this hangout. Scout around for girls, bounce ideas off each other, find out who we are. The age that I died and the age he is now—taking those steps together.

Herbie glanced into the living room and saw a very cute girl heading toward the stairway. "Check it out," he said to me. "Pretty nice, huh?"

"Very nice," I said. "Think she's got a friend for me?"

"She might," he said, "but she's leaving."

"Go after her."

"You think?"

"Do you know her?"

"Yeah. Her name's Hope. I talk to her in study hall."

"You make her laugh?" I asked.

"Always."

"That's a big first step."

He nodded. Pointed at me. "Be right back," he said, and he rushed toward the stairs. At the top step he stumbled and went flying face first to the bottom. I ran toward him as he fell, and he let out a little yelp and landed flat on his face. He tried to push himself up with his hands. He raised up slightly and we were suddenly awake, Herbie pushing himself up from the mattress, and me hovering there invisible and silent.

"Frank?" he said. He looked around his bedroom, felt his jaw, and realized that he'd been dreaming. "Oh shit, Frank. You're so frickin' real when I dream about you that it doesn't even occur to me that you're dead."

He got out of bed and turned on the light, then lay down on his back. "Son of a bitch," he whispered, shaking his head. "That really was you, wasn't it? I need to talk to you, Frank. For real. Not about washing dishes or picking up girls. You have to tell me you're all right, buddy. You have to let me know how I can help you."

I'm frustrated, too. The opportunity was there, but neither of us was alert enough to grab it. Still, you have to count the event as progress. We spoke to each other. We did.

Chapter Thirteen

Herbie spent the next two weeks on a rigid schedule of football practice, cross-country workouts, salad preparation and other kitchen duties at work, and deep, solid, rocklike sleep. He had time to ponder some of his life's bigger issues during runs through the woods and floor-mopping at the diner. These are things he figured out:

- Size doesn't matter all that much in football, unless you get hit. And you get hit at least once on every play.

- Falling into a zenlike rhythm while running can modify some of the pain, but it makes you drop way behind the others. Sucking it up and cursing at the pain makes you more competitive.

- Congealed ketchup does not come off in the dishwasher. You have to scrub it yourself.

- Athletic women are darn nice to look at, particularly runners.

- Interaction with a ghost can transfer certain types of energy and awarenesses to you if you pay attention. You might develop a sudden ability to see layers of the past in certain places. In a Main Street drugstore, for example, long-modernized and franchised and selling more hair-care products and magazines than cough remedies or aspirin, you might detect the presence of a wispy, heavily moustached former proprietor behind a long, low counter, working with balsam and opium and cod-liver oil. He's not really there, but he is.

   If you listen, you can hear rowdy laughter and strains of Irish music coming from within a store that sells used children's clothing and toys. It hasn't been a tavern in ninety years.

   You begin to see auras around your friends at times of heightened emotion, mostly light greens and yellows, but some of them dark and foreboding.

Herbie's exhaustion and the dry, relentless heat and his desire to figure out how best to take advantage of his next meeting with the ghost have kept him away from the cemetery for two weeks. There is a football game a week from Friday; school starts the following Tuesday, right after Labor Day. His first cross-country meet is also that week. His time is at a premium. But he is almost ready to go back.

Chapter Fourteen

Herbie has been figuring out his likely position on the cross-country team. It's up and down, of course; you have good days and bad days, days where every step up the wooded hills is a grind, other days where you just feel like you're flying without effort. There are five guys who are clearly better than he is, three or four more who usually outrun him in practice, and a handful of others who are more or less his equals. The top seven run varsity in major meets, but in duals the whole team runs together. He has a shot at varsity. He didn't come out for the sport to be anything less than that.

They've just finished a six-mile evening workout, and the coach has them lining up at the bottom of a short, steep hill below the soccer fields. "At the whistle you charge that hill," he says. "No letting up at the top; regain your form and sprint across the field. Then loop right back here, and we'll do it again."

"This sucks ass," Herbie says to the guy next to him, but he bolts up the hill at the whistle and finds himself ahead of all the others at the top. Ron easily hauls him down as they cross the soccer field, but only one or two others catch up. In a short test of speed and strength, he's one of the top guys on the team. But on longer runs he inevitably starts to fade. That kind of endurance takes a long time to develop. It's coming. He's improving. It's still very much summertime, but autumn is coming, and that's always been his season.

They run the hill five times, then jog back to the locker room. He stands under the shower for a good long time, letting the heat pound into his chest, eyes shut, breathing the steam, his hands up flat against the tiles. Beautiful exhaustion.

"You asleep there, Herbie?" says Reed Doherty, a senior and one of the top runners.

"Could be," Herbie says. "I'm beat. I could stand here all night."

"You don't wanna do that."

"Shit-yeah, I do."

"Nah. We got other plans."

"We do?" Herbie has known Reed a long time, but they've never been particularly close. Reed's got great looks but a crude act.

"Yeah. You got any shampoo?"

Herbie looks around. "Right over there," he says, pointing to a freshman in the corner of the shower room. "Hey, buddy, throw that bottle here."

The kid tosses it. Herbie takes a squeeze of it and hands the bottle to Reed. "So what's up?"

"Ellie and Diane." Two juniors from the girls' team. "I was talking to them. We want to hear about this ghost that's been following you. That's weird shit."

Herbie weighs this in his head for a few seconds, tilting his neck slowly from side to side. "Okay. What about it? And who told you that, anyway?"

"Gordon."

"I might as well advertise it on the radio."

"Don't worry. It won't go any farther than us. Anyway," Reed leans in closer, his soapy arm pressing into Herbie's, "maybe we can show them the scene of the crime, you know?"

Herbie rolls his eyes, grins a little. "It's scary stuff, man."

"That's what I'm counting on." Reed glances around, puts his hand up on Herbie's shoulder, his bare hip touching him, too. His aura is spiky and red. Herbie takes a step away. "Ellie's cool," Reed says. "I been wanting bad to get with her. She's been giving me vibes."

"So I'm with Diane?"

"If things go according to plan. You gotta make this work, though. It's got to be a scary scene."

Herbie rinses off. "It ain't a show, you know. I'll take you guys in there, but that doesn't mean anything will happen. And if it *does* happen, believe me, it's real."

"All right," Reed says. "Cool. They're meeting us outside. It's early yet. Let's go to the diner or something. You can get us free food?"

"No way. We only eat free when we're working."

"Well, maybe you can get us a deal."

"Don't count on it, pal."

Herbie steps out to his locker. Reed is a bit of a jerk, and he only wants to do this so he can make out with Ellie in the cemetery. Herbie will steer clear of any spots where he's likely to be haunted; no way is he sharing this with that guy. Diane, on the other hand, might be a different story. Herbie has admired her firm runner's legs, the way her dark hair bounces on her shoulders, her sly smile. The type I want for myself. Haunting in her own way. Worth knowing better.

"So, Herbie, what's good here?" Diane says as they slide into a booth at the diner. She's got a nice tan from lifeguarding at the town pool, and she's smiling at him as if she's amused to be here with him.

"Everything," Herbie says.

"Don't order anything with mayonnaise in it," Reed says. "You never know what these guys'll mix into it."

Diane looks surprised. "Like what?"

Herbie reaches across the table and smacks Reed's arm. "Nothing," he says. "The mayonnaise is fine."

Ellie raises her eyebrows. "You sure?"

Reed leans way forward and lowers his voice. "Tony told me they used to jack off in it back there."

"Oh, that is so gross," Diane says. She's looking at Herbie for confirmation or denial.

Herbie exhales and looks toward the ceiling. "That is such a crock of shit." He shakes his head and gives an embarrassed laugh. "Every restaurant in the world gets accused of that. It's ridiculous."

"It happens!" Reed says.

Herbie leans forward now. "It doesn't happen here."

Diane leans a bit toward the aisle, looking sideways at Herbie but keeping a tight smile. Her tongue peeks out from between her lips. "You sure?"

He exhales more loudly this time. "Think about how stupid that would be."

The waitress comes over to take their orders. Herbie goes first. "I want a turkey club with *extra* mayonnaise. Bring me a little cup of it on the side."

Diane starts to order. "Umm . . ." She giggles and looks over at Ellie, who's laughing harder. "What?"

She rolls her eyes and raises her hand as if to smack Ellie with the back of it. "I'll have the same thing as Herbie. And a Sprite."

Ellie orders a cheeseburger and a seltzer. "And put a little mayo on the roll," she adds.

Reed gets a roast beef sandwich. "With *mustard*." He shakes his head. "I warned you guys."

Herbie convinces them all to hang out by the Turkey Hill store for an hour or so. "Gotta wait until ten at the earliest," he says. The night is clear and warm but not too humid. Little chance of a thunderstorm. Not much likelihood of an encounter.

The Main Street bench in front of the store is empty, so the four of them squeeze on, with the boys on the ends and Diane next to Herbie. He's spent a lot of evenings on this bench, especially a couple of years ago when things were worst at home and he was avoiding every minute of it. These days he's either working, running, or sleeping in the evenings, or else he's in an Internet chat room discussing physics.

"So, does this thing sneak up on you and make eerie noises or what?" Diane asks.

"It's never made a sound," Herbie says. "I talk to it, but it doesn't talk back."

"Spooky." She bites down on her lip. She's got that

same grin as before, as if she can't believe she's hanging out with a guy like Herbie. He has a reputation for trouble, but nothing significant, and his looks are intriguing but not what girls think of as sexy. "Does it look human?" she asks.

"Yeah. It's a guy." He stops to think. "I've only seen it in human form one time, but it was a young guy, maybe nineteen or twenty. The other times it was just some kind of presence or energy. But I knew it was there, and it was definitely aware of me."

"Wow," she says.

"You girls better stay close to us," Reed says. "*Real* close."

Ellie folds her arms and rolls her eyes and says, "Puh-leeze," but she leans into Reed and smiles. "I'm shaking."

"I'll scare that sucker right back into his grave," Reed says. "He won't come back out till Halloween."

Herbie is thinking, *How did I get hooked up with this asshole?* He figures he should call the whole thing off, but then there's Diane, sitting leg-to-leg with him and smelling rather nice. She punches him in the knee. "Is this for real?" she whispers.

"You'll see," he whispers back. He looks straight ahead and nods. "It's real."

They walk all the way up North Main Street to the far entrance of the cemetery, past the library and the old mansions and the inns. They cross the bridge over the river and hook around on the back road that leads to the gate. The girls have been noticeably quiet as they approach; Reed has been keeping up his chatter.

They stop at the gate. The moon is half full but bright, and there are thin clouds and a breeze. Ellie says, "Wait."

"What's up?" Herbie asks.

"I'm not sure I want to do this."

"Oh, come on," Reed says. "Don't wimp out."

"I don't know," she says. "I've heard stories about this place. Herbie isn't the first one, you know."

"Geez," Reed says impatiently. "Let's just go a little ways." He couldn't care less about the ghosts; he wants a piece of her.

"A little ways," she says.

They walk about fifty yards, and Ellie stops again. She takes a seat on a low stone wall that runs parallel to the creek. The path is much darker ahead. "This is far enough for me," she says.

"Come on."

"No, I mean it. You guys go."

"I'll stay with you," Reed says before anyone can reply. He winks at Herbie. "Go ahead."

Herbie looks at Diane. She shrugs. "Let's go."

Herbie glances back. Reed has his arm around Ellie, and she's giggling again. *Fine with me,* Herbie thinks.

They keep their voices low and slow, just barely above a whisper.

They reach a turn in the path. "This way?" Diane asks.

"Yeah."

She takes hold of his arm, but he knows that's for security only. It feels good anyway. That whole side of his body gets warm.

"It's quiet," she says.

"Yeah. It always is in here. I don't think this place has changed in a hundred years."

"You think that's how old the ghost is?" she asks.

"No idea. But he died young, that's for sure. And he looked like pictures you see from way back."

"What was he wearing?"

"Nothing."

"Nothing?"

"No. He was naked. But not like a flasher or anything. Just, you know, like why would a ghost have clothes on?"

"I guess."

They walk in silence for a few minutes, approaching the upper loop.

"This is where I saw him," Herbie says, pointing toward the bridge. They stop and wait, looking intently. She moves a little closer, her shoulder pressing into his. He can smell her hair.

"Is he here?" she asks, sounding nervous.

He thinks for a moment, feeling the air. "I don't know," he finally says. "Usually he's farther in." He nudges her slightly with his elbow. "You want to keep going?"

She gives a soft, jittery laugh and says, "Sure."

He's hoping they'll see him, that he can share this with someone and know that it isn't in his head.

Nah. He knows that it's real. But he wonders if these others would see the ghost at all, or if he'd even appear when anyone else was around. He feels a personal connection with this ghost, has a belief that there is meaning behind these appearances.

He also sometimes wonders if he's going crazy.

"Are you scared?" she whispers.

"No. Are you?"

"Some. It's pretty spooky in here. I'd die if I had to go through here alone." She squeezes his hand, then keeps her hand in his.

"Let's sit down," he says.

"Where?"

"Pick a spot."

"No," she says. "You know this place. You pick one."

There are low walls around family plots, plenty of spots to rest. "I know a great place," he says. "This way."

They continue holding hands, and he leads her to the Appley plot, near the other end of the place. There are those marble benches, probably unused for a hundred years. He is not afraid at all.

"Nice spot," she says when they get there. She sits close to him, and he puts an arm up on the back of the bench, just barely touching her. They can hear the continual *twir-twir-twir*-ing of something—birds or baby frogs—and the chirping of crickets. Every minute or so comes the deep guttural croak of a bullfrog, and there are constant flashes of fireflies. Other than that, it's pitch dark.

"This guy," Herbie whispers, "the ghost? He looked... it was almost like I was looking in a mirror."

"Wow. Like an alter ego or something?"

He shakes his head. "No." He rubs his jaw with his free hand, presses his fingers against his mouth. "No. It was a different persona. Not something I generated. But maybe some distant relative or something. Looked a lot like my family. . . . You know Kevin?"

"The guy you work with?"

"Yeah."

"This isn't a mayonnaise story, is it?"

He lets out a loud laugh, then quickly looks around. "No. His grandmother knows all this stuff about ghosts. She lives right over there," he says, motioning toward the hill. "She said this ghost probably needs something from me."

"Like what?"

"I don't know."

Diane's aura is a pleasing transparent violet, clinging close to her body. There are pale flickers of orange, particularly when she leans into Herbie. He is very much aware of this.

"Do you see anything?" he asks.

"Like what?"

"Nothing. Energy? You see colors?"

She gives him a confused look. "Where?" she says a bit anxiously.

He shakes his head gently. "Nowhere. Not a ghost. I mean, do you ever sense color around someone?"

"I don't think so. I never thought about it."

Herbie notices that he is glowing with orange at the moment, and he's glad that she doesn't see it. An orange aura is sensual, the color of sexual arousal. It has occurred to him that being with a girl who can perceive that would be like getting an erection in calculus class and suddenly being called to the blackboard. Not an easy thing to hide.

They sit there for twenty minutes, growing more relaxed. She closes her eyes. "I'm tired," she says. "We ran a lot of miles this week."

"Tell me about it."

"Those hills at the end tonight were a bitch," she says. She opens her eyes. "That's our secret weapon, though. That's why our team is always so good. We work our asses off."

"I know it."

"You liking it?" she asks.

"Yeah. I like it fine. I can't wait to start racing."

"Me either." She looks around again, actually puts her hand on his knee. "Thought I heard something."

"Probably a squirrel. The ghost doesn't make any noise, remember?"

"Oh yeah." She giggles. "Anyway. You staying with football?"

"Yeah. What the hell. I'll get to play some. It'll keep me from getting bored."

"Right." She starts counting off on her fingers. "Football, cross-country, working at the diner, ghost hunting, *school.* . . . Sounds like you've got a *lot* of idle time."

"Yeah."

She doesn't put her hand back on his knee, but stays close anyway. They're quiet for several more minutes.

"Football in the morning?" she asks.

"Yep. And the afternoon, too."

"It's after eleven. You want to get going?"

"Sure."

They're near the River Road entrance, so they could be out of the cemetery quickly. He'd rather take the long way out.

"Want to walk back through?" he asks.

She glances toward the nearer entrance, then into the darker reaches ahead. "Okay," she says slowly. "I guess."

They walk a few yards and stop. There is a muffled, choking, crying sound coming from up ahead, but it's too dark to see quite from where. Diane grabs Herbie's hand and squeezes it so tight it hurts. "Ellie?" she says.

They take some very tentative steps and lean toward the sound, scanning the gravestones.

"This way," Herbie whispers, and he leads her toward the hill.

"What is that?" Diane asks.

"The wind?" Herbie says.

"No freakin' way, man."

Herbie is staring right at it, but it's obvious Diane can't see anything. A woman is on her knees, hunched over one of the tiny children's stones near the Dimmick plot, sobbing and wringing her hands. She's plump and about forty, and is unaware that she's being watched.

Diane lets go of Herbie's hand and squints, leaning forward. "Sounded like someone crying," she says.

"Probably a fawn," Herbie says, even though he can see otherwise. He knows that grave; it's from the 1870s. The foot-high stone has an image of a lamb carved on it, common back then with the deaths of children. SAMUEL, AGED 3 MOS.

The ghost lets out a higher wail, and Diane steps right into her, still not perceiving anything but the sound. Diane stumbles and falls to the ground, and the specter flares brightly. Herbie can see through it to Diane, wide-eyed and openmouthed, propped up on her hands as the woman slaps at her in anger.

Herbie lunges toward Diane, grabbing her shoulders and pulling her to her feet. They back away quickly and stop, arms around each other and staring at the grave as the ghost slowly dissolves into nothing.

They turn face-to-face and stare at each other in bewilderment.

"Holy shit," Herbie finally whispers.

"What? I didn't get hurt. I just slipped," Diane says.

"I know. You sure you're okay?"

"Absolutely." Diane is sweating and breathing hard. Herbie wipes her forehead with his fingers.

"Let's get the hell out of here," he says.

"Damn straight. Let's go."

"Holy shit."

"What was that, Herbie? That crying?" Diane says.

"I'll tell you later. Let's go."

He keeps an arm around her, and they head toward the nearer gate, the one that opens onto River Road. They keep looking around as they go, walking slowly at first but unclenching and beginning to run as they get back to the main path. In a minute they're out of the place, and Herbie breathes a huge sigh of relief. He gives a nervous laugh. "Unbelievable," he says.

"Was that a ghost?"

"Yeah. Some lady crying at her baby's grave," he says. "You couldn't see it?"

"No. I just heard that wailing."

"You, like, fell right into her," he says.

"Get out!" she says. "Jesus. My heart is racing."

They walk another hundred yards. "Sorry," he finally says.

"Why?"

"For getting you into this."

"No," she says. "Don't be sorry. This is fascinating."

"It's weird stuff, man."

"It's incredible. . . . That poor woman."

"Yeah, I know."

She puts an arm around his waist this time, and they walk in the middle of the road toward town. They say nothing for several minutes, listening to the river flowing past.

"Must be a lot of ghosts around here," Herbie says. He glances back toward the cemetery, and she turns and looks, too.

"Do you think they know each other?" she asks.

He thinks for a few seconds, biting down on his lower lip. "I don't think so," he says. "They just seem to be stuck. That lady? She's probably been crying there every night since her baby died, you know what I mean? She probably died in that spot out of grief."

"Oh god."

"My ghost, too. The young guy. I figure he's been searching for something forever. Like he's having a single thought over and over for however long he's been in there."

"So sad."

"And once every few decades somebody wanders in there at just the right second, with just the right weather conditions or whatever, and they make contact somehow, like we just did. And the ghost kind of wakes up and jolts out of that frozen-in-time state for just a couple of seconds and becomes aware of us. . . . I don't know how it works, man. They're just stuck there."

"Like they can't get past something?"

"Yeah. Like that." He stares into space for a moment, his mouth hanging open. "Maybe they're all waiting for me."

"You?"

"Seems like it," he says. "All of a sudden I'm seeing these things—ghosts and auras. . . . Why the hell are they latching onto me?"

"I don't know, Herbie." She gives him a smirky smile. "You're just special, I guess."

"Right." He shrugs. "Weird shit, man. Weird shit."

They've reached Park Street now and walk up past the YMCA toward Main Street. Herbie lifts the neck of his T-shirt to his face and wipes his sweaty upper lip. Diane removes her hand from his waist as they approach the more lighted area of town. She glances at her watch. "It's midnight," she says.

"The witching hour," he says with a smile. "Must be wild in there now."

"It was wild enough for me, thanks," she says. "That was incredible. I had no idea that I'd *fallen through* a ghost." She laughs a little and shakes her head. "Anyway," she says, "you said they didn't make any sound. I could definitely hear her crying, couldn't you?"

"Yeah. I said *my* guy didn't say anything. I don't know about any of the others."

"Right."

They stop at the corner of Main and Park, across from the Sturbridge Inn. Turkey Hill is a block away, and Herbie nods in that direction. "You want a soda or something?"

"I should get home. But yeah, why not? I'm already like two hours late. I'll call them."

"Good," he says. "I don't feel like being alone."

Herbie goes into the store to get drinks, and Diane goes to the pay phone.

"Okay?" he asks as they meet at the bench in front of the store.

"Yeah. They were pissed, but I told them I lost track of time. You'll walk me home?"

"Of course."

They sit on the bench and watch the sparse traffic going by.

"I'll never get to sleep after that," she says.

"I know the feeling."

"How do you deal with it?" she asks. "You've been going through this for weeks."

"I don't know. I've adjusted. The first couple times it happened, I wasn't really sure what was going on, you know? So it was scary and I'd have weird dreams, but I was so beat anyway that I managed to sleep when I had to. Tonight—that was by far the scariest thing that happened. I think I'll be up for quite a while."

"Me, too."

He sips his Mountain Dew and glances over at her, admiring again her toned body. She catches him looking. Sees his wry smile. "What?" she says.

"Nothing."

"What?" she says again, smiling back.

He shakes his head gently and shrugs.

A car goes by too quickly; four guys from the football team in an old green station wagon. "Herbie!" one of them yells.

Herbie gives a wave. They're gone.

"Can I tell you something?" he says.

"Sure."

"My brother's buried in there."

"Really?"

"Yeah. He died when I was little." Herbie uncaps the soda, twirls the white plastic cap between his thumb and first finger, and recaps it without drinking. "Cancer. He was so full of life, you know. I mean, he died so young. And I feel him trying to reach me sometimes. I even see him in dreams. And it seems like he's okay, but maybe that's just what I'm hoping for, and it isn't really true."

"Oh," she says. She rubs his wrist. "I'm sure he's all right, Herbie."

He nods, sniffs a little, and wipes his nose. "Yeah. But now I've seen these people who get stuck. They die, but not really? And I'm wondering, if they ever get unstuck—I mean, *when* they do—then what happens? Do they cease to exist, or do they move ahead to something else?"

"Like Heaven?"

"Yeah. Something like that. . . . If Frankie is trying to reach me, then where the hell is he? Is he in that cemetery with the rest of them? Has he been stuck there for the past ten years?"

"Wow. I hope not." She turns her upper body toward him and inches a little closer. She brushes a strand of hair behind her ear with her hand, then leans her elbow on the top of the bench. "I'm sure he's okay, Herbie. . . . Do you think he's the one you've been seeing? That guy?"

He shakes his head. "No. It's not him. But I guess what I'm worried about is maybe he doesn't have the strength to appear, you know? Like he's just lying in limbo and needs my help."

She's holding an unopened bottle of Coke in her palm, and she stares at it for a moment. "Before tonight I never would have believed it," she says. "But I see what you're worried about. I'm sure he was a really nice guy."

"He was like a big brother is supposed to be. You know, looking out for me, teaching me stuff, always doing stuff with me even when he could've been hanging out or whatever."

"Sounds really sweet. Really great."

"Yeah, he was. That's why I worry about him. He deserved better than dying at seventeen." Herbie turns his head slightly and eyes her. "I don't think he ever had a girlfriend," he says tentatively. "He never owned a car or went to college or had his own apartment. I just hope he's in a great place and he's happy. Not like these ghosts I keep seeing."

Herbie puts his face in his hands and leans forward on the bench. He lets out a sigh. "Sometimes I think I'm just fooling myself."

Herbie walks her home soon after, up North Main

Street and back toward the hospital to a small clapboard house on 16th Street. He says he'll see her tomorrow night at cross-country practice. She says, "Yeah. See ya then."

She stands on her front porch and watches until he's gone from sight. And she sleeps well that night, despite everything that happened.

Chapter Fifteen

Late afternoon. The weather has shifted—a strong cooling breeze, little humidity, a teasing hint of autumn in the air.

"Hit that hole!" the coach yells as Herbie grabs a handoff and darts forward. The seam is tiny, but he breaks through it. Big Phil Weiss gets a hand on him, but Herbie pulls loose and dodges past a linebacker. An arm around his waist keeps him from gaining momentum, and the safety comes up and brings him down. Five-yard gain.

Herbie hops up and jogs to the huddle. This is just an in-squad scrimmage at the end of practice. Coach is calling the plays. Herbie's at tailback. "Thirty-five," Coach says, another play for Herbie.

Gordon is in at quarterback. He's driven the team from its own twenty to near midfield. Herbie's had four carries for about fifteen yards, but this is against a very tired defense. Gordon takes the snap and hands off to Herbie, who cuts off tackle and gets through the hole cleanly. He stutters left, then uses that amazing acceleration to take off toward the sideline. The safety freezes, and Herbie gives a little jive step, racing into the clear. The blocks have been in his favor, and that whole side of the field is wide open. In a matter of seconds he is ahead of all pursuers, and he sprints down the field into the end zone.

"Beautiful," Coach says as he jogs back. Gordon lifts him in a bear hug, and other guys smack his helmet. Just a practice session, but a breakthrough nonetheless.

Coach blows his whistle, and the team gathers around. "Five laps, then hit the showers. Same practice times tomorrow. Good effort."

Herbie starts to run with the rest of them, but Coach calls him over. "Listen, you have cross-country practice later?"

"Yeah. In about an hour."

"Okay. Skip the laps then. Nice job out there. You'll get some work in the games. You're quick."

"Thanks. Felt good out there today."

"Looked good, too."

He jogs to the locker room and strips off his gear. No sense showering, since he's got a long run ahead of

90

him, but he washes his hands and face at the sink. He downs a quart of water and eats an apple and a banana while sitting in front of a fan outside the trainer's office. He glances outside a few times to see if anyone's by the track yet.

After a while a van pulls up over there, and he sees Diane get out. He tosses the banana peel in a trash basket and goes to his locker for his running shoes. Football teammates are coming in by now. Phil grabs his shoulders from behind.

"Hey, big man," Herbie says.

Phil squeezes his shoulders. "Give me some of that lightning," he says with a grin. "Give me that speed and I'd be in the NFL, baby."

"You'd be a dangerous man, that's for sure."

"You're a little mosquito, Herbie. I'm batting at ya and trying to knock you down. You're too damn quick."

"That's fear!" says Gordon, whose locker is next to Herbie's. "He knows what would happen if you catch him."

"Yeah," says Herbie. "Save your big hits for Pocono."

"We'll kick their asses," Phil says. He spreads his arms to address the room. "We'll kick their asses!"

Someone turns on the stereo, and Phil starts dancing. It's of little concern right now that the Scranton

Rich Wallace

paper has Pocono ranked second in Northeastern Pennsylvania in its preseason poll. Sturbridge went 2–7 last fall. Herbie puts on a fresh T-shirt and heads for the door.

Diane is stretching on the side of the track when Herbie jogs over. I feel something like a surge of energy go through me, an almost physical yearning.

She sees Herbie approaching and smiles. He raises his hand to wave and says, "Boo."

She laughs. "Boo yourself." She shakes her head. "I still can't believe last night, Herbie."

"Wild shit, huh?"

"Oh my god," she says.

"I know."

She puts her hand on his chest, just below his shoulder. "Listen, I don't want to tell anybody what happened. Okay?"

He nods. "Yeah. I'm keeping my mouth shut this time."

"I already told Ellie nothing happened. She wouldn't get it anyway."

"Yeah," Herbie says. "And Reed . . . he had one thing in mind, and it wasn't exactly spiritual."

"No kidding. Ellie said he was all over her as soon as we left. I mean, get to know her a little before you try to jump her."

"Yeah."

She runs her finger from his chest to his navel. "Talk to the girl for a while, at least." She smiles. "That was really nice last night."

"It was."

"Let's try it again sometime," she says.

"Yeah. Anytime. Tonight even."

"I would," she says with a frown, "but I can't. My mom's picking me up after practice, and we're driving to my aunt's over in Dunmore."

"Tomorrow then?"

"Yeah," she says. "After practice. We can hang out first, until it gets dark."

"Sounds good. I'll bring a flashlight."

"Should I bring anything?" she asks.

"Like what?"

"Some refreshments?"

"Sure, if you want to," he says. "Anything you want."

"I'll surprise you."

"I can't wait."

Chapter Sixteen

There is a dark zone where the more Earthbound of us dwell for however long it takes us to move on. I have denied to myself that I am stuck in this zone, but things Herbie said to Diane have forced me to face up to this fact.

I am as ignorant of the next level of the afterlife as you are of this one, but I've learned that there are many levels of existence. As one moves forward—and moving forward requires wisdom and experience— each successive realm becomes less physical and more spiritual. That final level is pure spirit; physical and personal needs have been shed, and what is left is pure energy. That is how we began. That is where we eventually will return.

In the beginning, as they say, the universe was a tiny throbbing dot of pure energy. The big bang turned some of that energy into matter, space, and time.

Energy can never be destroyed. And all matter eventually returns to a state of energy. That is where we are headed.

The zone I am in, where I have been since my physical death, is not dramatically different from the "living" world I inhabited for seventeen years. Here we are still as much matter as energy, even though we are no longer with our bodies.

There are souls who remain in this dark zone seemingly forever, not seeking knowledge, not seeking growth, merely replaying parts of their lives or trying to reconnect with those "below." It is not at all unusual (but it is spiritually stifling) to stay here for an extended time period, but most of us eventually move on.

There are those, I am told, who do not even "land" here, but enter the afterlife a plane or two higher. Those are the rare ones who achieved more enlightenment while on Earth; they've already learned the lessons we apparently need to learn on these lower levels. It took me a long time to even realize that I had lessons to learn. It is only recently that I became aware that I was avoiding the steps I need to take.

It is not easy.

My grandfather has awakened. He knows me. He remembers his time on Earth; he still loves his family but is eager to move on. He waits for my grandmother, who is still "alive." He tells me stories I can't remember from my earliest childhood, of days in the park, feeding bread to the ducks. He shares with me my family's sadness surrounding my death. But he is at peace. He has few regrets about his days on Earth, few unfilled needs or desires. So he can move on. And he will, but not until my grandmother arrives.

That's the result of a long and rewarding life.

So what about me? I am not quite "stuck" in the sense that Eamon Connelly is, in the way that Herbie feared I might be. But I am unwilling to move on. Too many things I'd have to leave behind. Too many things I don't have yet.

Herbie is a virgin. He has some physical experience with girls, some make-out sessions at parties or in parked cars. Not many. About the same amount I'd done at his age. He's never been in love, and neither have I.

Ten years I've been dead. A blink of the eye in the scope of eternity. But an eternity in and of itself when you go through it the way that I have. Imagine yourself, freethinking and intelligent, unable to connect with anyone for a decade. To wander lonely and unseen, watching and yearning. Trapped—not trapped *in* a body, but trapped *without* one. Do you think passion expires? Do you think you stop wanting a physical connection, to run your hands over the body of a partner, to caress her shoulders, her back, her butt, her waist; to taste her lips; to enter her and share with her that incredible moment of release? Do you think that goes away?

Imagine watching as your little goddamn brother raises orange auras around a sexy young athlete as they huddle together in the dark of the cemetery. Imagine knowing where that eventually may lead. Imagine knowing that you'll never experience that savory anticipation, that physical buildup until you feel you might explode, that sharing of passion and desire, and especially that ability to quench it!

Trapped? Yes, I am trapped. How can I ever move on when I have not achieved the single thing I most desire? How can I ever rest? You think it's easy? It's hell!

Chapter Seventeen

Herbie heads for the cemetery late that evening, keyed up in anticipation of the next night's visit with Diane. He'd taken a shower, let off some of the tension, but Herbie's the kind of guy who likes to scout things out, to make a run-through before the main event.

He walks down Park Street a bit before midnight, planning an easy jog through the cemetery. But he never gets there. As he turns onto River Road, he catches a flash of light on his periphery. He stops and turns. He is below the cliff. Across from him is the steep wooded slope, climbable but rocky and dark. There is an easy path that loops around the hill and winds its way to the top, but one can also follow a more or less straight ascent through a washed-out gulley that rushes with water in a storm but is usually dry, as it is tonight.

It's been months since Herbie has been on top of the

cliff, and he suddenly wants to be up there. The view of the town is complete and comforting, down in its own little valley between this hill and a mirroring one on the other side.

So he begins to climb, grasping small trees to pull himself along, feeling his way over rocks and downed branches.

And there's that flash again, ahead of him. Eamon Connelly, looking back at him, eyes wide. Eamon beckons Herbie with a sweeping motion of his hand, then turns and continues climbing. Herbie swallows hard and continues, too, letting Eamon get farther ahead.

Halfway up, Herbie looks down at the town, mostly dark, single-family homes surrounding the business district, which itself is only a block deep and six blocks long. Only Main Street is lit at this hour. He squints and determines that there's no one hanging out by Turkey Hill.

Eamon is climbing steadily ahead, and the path up there looks wet from back where Herbie is. But it's dry where Herbie is climbing.

Eamon reaches the steeper, bare rock face that juts thirty feet or so up to the top. The shale here is brittle, but there are a multitude of hand- and footholds in the rock—holes and ledges where one can insert a toe or some fingers and get a grip, slowly and carefully pulling your way up. I want to holler at Herbie to head back down, to not risk this climb. I have a sudden feeling of terror for him. But there's nothing I can do to stop him.

Herbie leans against a tree and looks straight up. Eamon is moving quickly up that sheer face, and Herbie is startled to see that rain is coming down and lightning is flashing, though he is not getting wet at all.

And suddenly Eamon is falling, and Herbie takes a quick step back to avoid being hit. Herbie slides several feet and grabs at the dirt, stopping himself as Eamon lands above him with a thud.

Herbie hears Eamon's pain-ridden cry and the cracking of bone against rock. He scrambles to his feet and scuttles over to the spot where Eamon hit. But there is nothing there. No body; no ghost. Not even the echo of Eamon's cry.

"Shit" is all Herbie can say. He sits on the dirt for a few minutes, catching his breath. Then he starts back toward town in a hurry.

I stay behind. How many times has Eamon tried to make that climb in the past hundred years? How many times has he failed?

That moment of his falling is so emotionally charged, so intense. I felt it with Eamon, I must admit. That helpless grasping—finding nothing there. Like the absence of strength in a cancer-infested body. That instant of panic as you fall through the air—fighting with everything you've got to avoid that plunge into darkness. The searing, all-encompassing pain as the body crashes into rock. I felt it.

I felt it as Eamon felt it. Even without a body, I could feel it.

Chapter Eighteen

This is the final day of double sessions for the football team. There's a game on Friday night. School starts next week. For Herbie, it has been a week of triple sessions—conditioning and skill development in the mornings with the football team, full-contact scrimmaging in the steamy afternoons followed by wind sprints. An hour or so to catch his breath and refuel, then a grueling evening session with the runners.

State athletic-participation rules have been bent, if not broken, but officially he has been excused from the afternoon football sessions. Unofficially, he hasn't missed even one.

Today it was easy. Given the anticipation of a cozy night in the cemetery with Diane, this guy can take anything. A few bruising hits, a dozen or so fifty-yard sprints. Hell, what's that? He's got a supply of adrenalin that won't stop pumping.

straight to her shoulders. Her T-shirt says QUEEN FOR A DAY, and she's wearing leather sandals and khaki shorts. She gives him a sassy smile—as much a pucker as a smile—and says, "Hey. I'm starving."

"Me, too. You want pizza or what?"

"Okay," she says. "Better load it up with stuff, though."

"Sure."

"Let's go to Foley's. They have a good jukebox."

So they go and eat and hang out there afterward to kill time until dark, listening to old songs by Meat Loaf and the Police and R.E.M. and drinking a pitcher of water. She tends to talk about her body, not in a sexual way but in the way that runners do—minor ailments like Achilles tendon soreness or the occasional side stitch, but mostly the strength she seems to be gaining, the ability to continue charging after a hill or to maintain a racing pace a bit longer than last season. His contribution could be the beginning of athlete's foot—some splitting and itching between the toes—which he does not mention, or a more powerful sprinting mode, which he does.

"I can't wait to go full speed down the field for like fifty yards and knock a guy flat on his ass on a kickoff," he says. "I'm definitely looking forward to that."

She comes up to him before the evening workout, grabs his wrist and pulls him toward her mouth. "Got a nice surprise," she whispers.

He's blushing. "Like what?"

"Something tasty. A little razz."

"Yeah. Where is it?"

"It's in a water bottle in my locker. Not much, but enough to give us a buzz."

"Cool. What's in it?"

"You know. A mixture. A little red wine, a little white. Some brandy. Whatever bottles were open and wouldn't look too depleted if I took some."

"I got ya."

"It'll be fun," she says. "And scary."

"Yeah. Scary. You've been touched by a ghost. That changes things."

"I can't wait. That was awesome the other night. I can't even imagine what'll happen in there tonight." She winks at him and jogs off to join the girls' team.

He watches her go, admiring her aura and the rest of her.

I watch her, too.

I know of others who died young, who passed suddenly in crumpled Fords or in blazes or from gunshots, or those whose bodies were slowly ravaged by cancer or other diseases, as mine was. I have avoided them.

My death was not unexpected, but I fought it to the final moment. My last utterance was the beginning of a scream that faded as quickly as I did.

I was not in much pain to speak of. I was weak, but I fought like hell. I had far too much still to do.

I kept trying to fit back into my body, to "return." It wouldn't take me. What was left of it weighed seventy-seven pounds.

There was no "reawakening" after death; I never quite lost consciousness. I was just suddenly aware that I was dead. So there was panic, those attempts to return. Then a deep, deep sadness. Not denial. I knew what had happened. But I mourned for myself. I watched my mom enter the hospital room and gently stroke my forehead, bend to me and sweetly kiss my cheek, tell me she loves me and she'll always love me and will see me in Heaven.

My father, dumbfounded. Staring at me, shutting his eyes. Opening them and fighting back tears.

Little Herbie just bawling.

And the realization that I was now on two planes at once—very much aware of the physical, earthly realm; very much still there. And above me, all around me, in fact, right behind me and under me, something else. Something vast and dark and seemingly empty and

infinite. Something like space. A realm I fe destined to float through forever if I ever let I had here below.

If I ever let go.

I still haven't.

Herbie runs with spirit this evening—an workout of various paces through the woods the soccer fields, charging the hills, throwing second bursts of speed on the flatter section maintaining a steady rhythm on the stretche ment past the tennis courts and the baseball cooler this evening; the air is noticeably less stays in the lead pack for most of the worko ning to believe that he belongs there. From tin they cross paths with the girls' team, so lean and upright.

"Meet you right here?" he says to her afte driveway behind the locker rooms.

"Yeah," she says. "I need about twenty mi

He takes a deep, hot shower and drinks a orange Gatorade. Puts on a new black T-shirt. a couple of small zits in the mirror and decide leave them alone. He gargles, combs his hair, a a big inhale and lets it out.

Diane's got her hair down and it's wet,

She smiles and kicks his shin very gently under the table. "Tough guy."

He shrugs. "That's me," he says in a way that sounds both confident and self-deprecating. "I ain't scared of nothing."

At dusk they walk toward the cemetery. She has the bottle in a small paper bag. She stops and twists off the cap when they're a few feet past the gate. She takes a swig and wipes her mouth. "Tasty," she says. She licks the corner of her lips.

She hands him the bottle—one of those thin, clear plastic water bottles, which contains about eight ounces of pale maroon liquid. Herbie tilts it to his mouth and drinks.

A woman passes them walking a black Labrador, and they nod and say good evening. It will be fully dark soon, and Herbie needs to get them deeper into the place where it is secluded and eerie. He is not thinking much about ghosts. He leads her to a spot near the top of the hill, under the tallest pine trees, where a few narrow slate steps are built into the dirt, leading to the Hopkins family plot, circa 1860s.

They sit close together and talk about running and music, and he introduces her to more of his theories about ghosts and the universe and other planes of existence. "You wouldn't believe how many wackos there are in these physics chat rooms, even the ones run by Stanford and MIT. But there's some brilliant people, too. Really interesting ideas on what this is all about," he says, waving his hand toward the sky.

"And ghosts?" Diane asks, inching closer.

"Well, on the more serious sites, you get some harsh criticism if you bring up things like that or UFOs," he says. "There are sites for that stuff, but they're pretty trashy, on the level of the *National Enquirer*."

An hour passes as they slowly empty the bottle. They sit tighter. She reaches toward his ear and runs her fingers down his neck and across his shoulder. "How cool," she says.

"What?"

"I can see your colors, Herbie. Like you said."

"Like what?"

"Your aura," she says. "It's yellow and a soft purple. With flashes of orange." She caresses his knee.

"I told you," he says. "After I got touched by a ghost, I developed these sensitivities. I started seeing things I never knew existed. Now it's happening to you."

He shifts his leg to increase the contact area. "People think it's so New-Agey and weird," he says.

"It's just energy. That's all anything is. Most people can't see it, so they just don't believe it."

Diane's voice sounds teasing now, playful. "So what are the orange flashes about?" she asks.

"Well . . ."

"I think I know," she says.

"Yeah?"

"Yeah." She shifts her body quickly and straddles him, sitting face-to-face, her butt on his thighs. She smiles and leans in, bringing her mouth down to his, gently stroking his lips with hers.

This activity keeps them busy for two hours. There is no haunting this evening, but lots of transference of energy. He walks her home. Both are happy.

Herbie grabs a can of Coke when he gets to the house and reads a note from our mom: *I have to go to Scranton tomorrow. Leaving early and back late. Eat the leftover chicken. Love you. Mom.* He climbs the stairs to his room and logs on to the Internet and goes into the message board. He scrolls through the evening's disjointed postings:

rsingh *8/28 22:55* You tell me, please, how did the universe start from nothing? How does a photon's worth of energy--Less than a speck! Barely an idea!--explode into an entire universe? You can't explain it. It's either by chance or by God. Take your pick.

shaddo *8/28 22:57* If starlight bends around the sun, then photons must have mass, right?

MSR640 *8/28 22:58* No. Photons are pure energy. Gravity affects energy. No mass required.

chipper *8/28 23:01* Sanji, you suk. Why'd you post your whole stupid thesis here? This is a CHAT room, dik.

cosmo-not *8/28 23:04* You all spend so much energy on why we are here and what came before the Big Bang. There IS no general reason why we are here. The reason is within each INDIVIDUAL. "We" are here because anything that CAN happen, eventually WILL happen, including life and intelligence. And an AFTERLIFE. There is no afterlife. Not yet. There won't be until we create one. One day we will. We'll figure it out and we'll generate it. There's no hand of God out there, boys. No Heaven until we get smart enough to create one.

rsingh *8/28 23:06* And then "we" become God, cosmo? Not so. He already exists. He is why we are here!

androyd *8/28 23:08* Cosmo, yoove got to be a chik, with all THOSE CAPITAL LETTERS, but yu make some sense on the afterlife. And just as there is no "after" in afterlife, there really was no such thing as "before" before the Big Bang. Not in the sense that we know it.

cosmo-not *8/28 23:10* GUYS use caps, too, androyd. But yes, I'm female. Before long, we will have come up with a way to capture the spirit (soul, whatever) at the time of death and allow it to exist briefly, independent of the body. The first documented afterlives will be short-lived (seconds) but indisputable. Over time, we'll lengthen it to years, both because of our own experience and because the recent dead will be able to help us. We'll get feedback from them. They'll tell us what they need in order to continue. I don't think there will ever be an infinite afterlife, but we WILL create a whole new level of existence.

androyd *8/28 23:12* "Imagine there's no Heaven. It's easy if you try."

cosmo-not *8/28 23:13* NO! Imagine that there IS one. That's how such things get started.

Herbie thinks for a while, then begins to type. Eventually he sends this instant message:

goalie *8/29 00:37* Cosmo-not, you still awake? I have mentioned ghosts in this forum before and been shouted down (even by you). But now you are talking about ghosts yourself. What is that momentary "spirit" you expect to capture and release but a ghost? They do exist. I've seen them. I've been touched by them. I have heard them. There IS another level of exis- tence, and it's a sad one. What I see are spir- its who are stuck in one place--stuck both in time and locality, who seem to be searching for that one action or event that will release them from the limbo. I know about them. I know that

they exist. What I don't know is about everyone else that's died. Those that didn't get
stuck. Are they gone forever or are they alive
on some higher plane? When these ghosts finally get past some barrier, do they simply expire
or do they go on to something better?

cosmo-not *8/29 00:39* I'm here. Relax. You know
the answer. The answer is that we don't know.
So we live for NOW. WE aren't stuck. (And who
are these ghosts? Why are they haunting YOU?)

goalie *8/29 00:40* They're in a cemetery. And
actually, I seek THEM out. They're fascinating.
Scary, but so far harmless.

cosmo-not *8/29 00:41* Kule. So what do YOU
want from THEM?

goalie *8/29 00:42* Some kind of assurance, I
guess. One, that life goes on--not as a ghost,
but beyond that. And two, that my brother made
it through. He died when I was a kid. I have
this fear that he's stuck somewhere, too. That
he's nearby, but that he can't quite connect
with me. I feel him trying to reach me.

cosmo-not *8/29 00:43* You think the cemetery ghosts can help you connect?

goalie *8/29 00:43* No. They can't even help themselves. Like you said, they need help. But that level of "afterlife existence" you hope to generate is already there. Maybe that's where we start. If we can interact with ghosts in some meaningful way, then maybe we can begin to extend that afterlife, as you mentioned.

cosmo-not *8/29 00:44* Maybe. Where is this cemetery?

goalie *8/29 00:46* Pennsylvania. But I already believe in the afterlife. I mean, if ghosts exist (They do! I'm no wacko) then why is it such a stretch to believe in some sort of "heaven" beyond that? The whole fact that we're here, that this universe exists, that it holds intelligent beings, that I'm sitting here typing this message and even pondering the notion of existence and spiritual life and afterlife is so wildly improbable--yet so indisputably real--that I can't wholly doubt the possibility of ANYTHING. What could be more bizarre than

what we already KNOW exists? We take for grant-
ed all that we see and experience. Think about
how incredibly unlikely it is. The simple fact
of our existence is far more unlikely than the
possibility that it would continue--beyond
physical death--in some realm that we haven't
yet tapped into.

Chapter Nineteen

Home game. Bright lights. The bleachers are packed.
The new season begins.

Herbie jogs a few steps in place. He looks at his
teammates, spread out from sideline to sideline, waiting for him to kick off. He takes a giant breath and shuts
his eyes, then opens them and looks up the field
toward the goalposts. He raises his hand and brings it
down, moving forward and hammering the ball with
his foot.

Helmets and shoulder pads crash, and a Pocono
guy is coming toward him, his assignment to take out
the kicker. Herbie dodges and scoots left, guessing
which way the kick-return man will be coming. He
hears voices rising in the crowd, an excitement that
adds to the chaos. And then he sees the ball carrier
behind a wall of blockers, streaking toward the sideline as sky-blue Sturbridge jerseys go sprawling to the

ground. Herbie is hit in the side but keeps his balance, and the return man is even with him with a clear field toward the end zone. There's a blocker between them, and Herbie needs to outrun them both somehow. If he can get past the blocker, he can catch the ball carrier before he scores, but no, they see that too clearly. A clean, low block knocks Herbie's feet from under him, and he goes flat onto the turf.

The game is sixteen seconds old, and already it's six to nothing.

"Shit!" he says, climbing back up, yanking a hunk of sod from his face mask. He looks at the Pocono players, mobbing the return man. Herbie smacks himself on the helmet and jogs off the field. "Son of a bitch," he mutters.

The game is brutal; Sturbridge is totally outmanned. Herbie punts four times in the first half and makes two touchdown-saving tackles. The third punt is blocked, and Herbie gets smothered by two giant linemen. The fourth punt is run back for a score. At halftime it's 35–0.

The head coach looks around the locker room at his players, sitting there shell-shocked, their backs against the lockers. "That's one hell of a good team," the coach says after a minute. "We're gonna take it one play at a time, fellas. Let's make a good showing in the second half, then we regroup and move forward. They're very quick off the ball, and that's putting it mildly. We're going to try something a little different on offense, get a bit more speed in there. Quicker counts, more motion, short passes in the flat."

Herbie goes in at wingback on the first offensive series of the half, carrying off-tackle for a yard before being brought down in a heap of red-and-white jerseys. He carries again for a two-yard loss. After an incomplete pass, he drops back to punt.

He gets off a nice one, angling it toward the sideline. It bounces out of bounds, and he breathes easy.

Pocono plays its second string for most of the second half, but they get three more touchdowns anyway. Herbie goes in at tailback late in the fourth quarter, and Gordie Shuler is at quarterback.

Herbie rushes straight up the middle for three yards, then off tackle for seven. Gordie completes a short pass near the sideline. They call time-out and huddle up.

"Seven seconds left," Gordie says. "Everybody go deep. On two."

Gordie grabs Herbie's sleeve as they break the huddle. "I'm pitching it to back you," he says. "Follow me around the end."

He takes the snap and flips it to Herbie, who is already moving toward the sideline. Gordie dashes out and throws a great block, and Herbie sees running room to his right. He cuts upfield and reaches full acceleration, hurdling over one downed defender and breaking into the clear.

He crosses midfield and races desperately toward the end zone, but several Pocono players are in pursuit. One gets a hand on him near the thirty, slowing him down and pinning him in at the sideline. He gets another ten yards before being thrown to the turf. Two guys come down on him. The gun sounds. Game over. Herbie is the team's leading rusher: fifty-eight yards on five carries, most of it in that last frantic dash.

He hooks up with a group of people after the game, including Gordie, Diane, and Reed. Reed takes him aside as they walk up Main Street. "Looks like I made the wrong choice," Reed says.

"About what?"

"Diane. Sounds like I gave you the horny one. I didn't get anywhere with Ellie."

"Eat shit," Herbie says. "You think it's as simple as that?"

"What, like you would have done better with Ellie?"

"I ain't saying that." Herbie just shakes his head.

"You're a frickin' bonehead. This isn't worth talking about."

"Yeah, well just remember, I set you up. You owe me."

Diane has dropped back to join them now. "You owe him what?" she asks.

"He loaned me a couple of bucks the other night," Herbie says quickly. "I told you you'd get it by tomorrow," he says to Reed. "Now screw off."

Herbie and Diane lag behind as they walk toward the pizza place.

"Holy shit," he says, changing the subject. "They were fast as anything. I got bruises up and down my whole body."

"It wasn't pretty," she says.

"We suck," he says. She doesn't argue.

"I'm so frickin' beat," he says. "We got cross-country practice tomorrow?"

"Nine o'clock. You have football?"

"Yeah. At eight. No pads. They don't want us hanging out after the games, so they make it early. He said I can leave to run if I have to."

"You gonna?"

"Probably. I'm supposed to do football on Monday, Wednesday, and Thursday, since the cross-country meets are usually Tuesdays and Saturdays. All the football games are Friday nights. I don't know when the hell I'm supposed to just *run*. I guess I'll do laps during football practice."

"You could give up football. It doesn't look like much of a season anyway."

"Nah," he says, yawning. "I like it. It's not as if my whole identity is tied up in it like some of these guys."

She puts her hand on his shoulder. "You should get home to bed. We can get together tomorrow night."

"I know."

"You don't have to work tomorrow, do you?"

"No. I cut back just to Sundays for now. No way I could keep up that pace with school starting. I'd be a basket case."

She flicks up her eyebrows. "Hit the cemetery tomorrow night?"

"Sounds good to me."

"All right then." She kisses him. "I'm gonna get pizza with those guys. I'll get home on my own. See ya in the morning."

"Right." He looks over at Reed, then back at Diane. He figures he's got nothing to worry about. Diane goes into Foley's, and Herbie keeps walking. When he reaches the traffic light he hesitates briefly, looking up the street toward home. Instead he turns and walks down Park

Street toward the cemetery. It's been a while since he was in there alone.

I speed ahead to get there before he does. I have come to a big realization that should have been obvious. When Herbie and Diane were touched by ghosts, they gradually became more aware of each other's auras. I think if I can somehow connect with Eamon, then perhaps my energy field would be enhanced as well. Maybe they'd be able to see me.

There are several ghosts that haunt the Dyberry Cemetery, but most of them are usually inactive. It takes a lot of energy to re-form, so most of them don't wander very far. Eamon has been stirred up this summer because of Herbie's presence; others can appear only in just the right atmospheric conditions or when the opportunity arises to latch onto a particularly kinesthetic person. Otherwise they lie dormant, sometimes for decades.

I make several circuits of the place, but for the life of me I can't stir up a ghost. Herbie is making his way slowly along the path, at peace but wary, showing a little fear. He is headed toward my grave site, so I go there and wait.

My mom has recently placed flowers by the grave, and the grass here is thick and healthy, shaded as it is from the summer sun by the hemlock several feet away. My stone is nearly square, cut from brownish marble with a shiny face; my name, FRANK HERBERT, carved in block letters, with the dates, and simply, *At rest.*

I look up, and Herbie is standing there, very still, leaning toward the grave and inhaling. He kneels and runs his open palm over the grave, about six inches above the ground, within inches of where I'm perched on the gravestone.

"Is that you, Frank?" he says. "That warmth?"

"I'm here," I say, but he doesn't hear me. I move to touch his shoulder, but he shows no sign of feeling me. Yet he is aware. He feels a warmth, he has spoken to me. "Up here," I say, but his attention is toward the earth.

He's on his knees now, his face near the ground. "I feel you, Frank," he says. "I feel your heat. Unless somebody just pissed here." He laughs. Then he looks up at the stone. "It's okay, buddy," Herbie whispers. "I miss you, Frank. We all miss you. I'm playing football—we got our asses kicked tonight like you wouldn't believe. I've even got a girlfriend now, I think." He slides his hand over the face of the stone, over my name. "We're all good, Frank. . . . I know you can hear me."

"Herbie!" I say. I say it sharply. He looks up and

looks around, as if there's some recognition, but I don't think he quite heard me.

"Herbie!" I shout it this time, but he doesn't move or respond.

He stays there for a few more minutes, then stands and pats my stone. "I'll be back," he says. "Soon. Tomorrow night maybe. You can meet Diane."

Herbie stands and looks at the grave for a minute or so. "I know you're here, Frank," he says. "Thanks for seeing me through."

He starts to walk away, then stops and turns. "Hey," he says. "Remember when I was about four and I got those new cowboy boots? You walked me over to Grampa's so I could show them off, and I stepped in dog shit? A big hunk of it stuck right to the front! I was pissed." He laughs. "You hosed off the boots when we got there and set 'em in the sun to dry. You said that's why they made cowboy boots in the first place, to keep cow shit off their toes. I've always remembered that."

He stands there another minute, grinning in my direction. "Keep the shit off your toes," he says. "I won't ever forget that." He points toward me with his thumb up and first finger out, like a pistol. "Don't you ever forget it either."

Chapter Twenty

The head football coach's mood is very different this morning. He starts chewing them out right away about their execution and their attitude. Where's all that conditioning, the fundamentals we've been stressing, the desire? "You guys packed it in after that opening kick-off got ran back," he says. "What the hell was that all about?"

They go out and run wind sprints for an hour. Everybody's pretty somber and sore. They get yelled at again after the running.

Herbie finds the cross-country coach at about 9:45, up by the track. All the runners are out on the course.

"I'll get in a workout this afternoon," Herbie says.

"I see," the coach says with a frown.

"I'm wiped out."

Coach studies his fingernails, not looking at Herbie. "I'm not surprised," he says. "You're spreading yourself too thin."

"I can handle it."

Now Coach looks him straight in the eye. He's a poker-faced guy in his forties, lean like a runner and all business. Teaches history. "This sport takes total commitment, my friend." He points to the lettering on the pocket of his golf shirt: *Sturbridge Cross-Country.* "This is a championship program. We dish out beatings like the one your football team took last night. You want to be a part of it, you have to be around every day. Otherwise you're just on the fringe."

Herbie nods slowly. He knows he has every right to do both sports. And he plans to continue. "I'm committed," he says. "Believe me, I'll run this afternoon."

"We've got a meet on Wednesday, as you know. I think you can help this team, but I won't hand you anything. Dual meets you'll compete like everybody else, but you won't be in the Saturday invitationals unless you're squarely in the top five in the duals. You can't run JV as a senior, and—all things being equal—I'll choose a full-timer for varsity every time."

Herbie stares over at the track, biting on his lip. "Okay," he finally says. "Coach, I'm not quitting football.

I like it. I think I can make your varsity, too. I expect to."

"Well," he says, pointing toward the woods, "as far I can tell, my varsity is out there running right now. You're supposed to be here on Saturdays. That was part of the deal."

"I know it. I'm sorry. I couldn't get out of football this morning."

"That's your choice," he says. "But I've got choices to make, too."

Herbie sits in the bleachers to wait for Diane. She comes up to him after her run and squeezes his arm. "You get any sleep?" she asks.

"Not a whole lot," he says.

"Too bad, huh?" She squints at him a bit. "You all right?"

"Yeah. Just been getting reamed by coaches all morning. Lots of fun."

"Poor baby," she says. She lifts the edge of her T-shirt and wipes the sweat from her face, exposing her abs and her navel. "You still up for tonight?"

"Of course. I'll sleep this afternoon."

"You look angry."

"Well, I got my ass handed to me twice today," Herbie says. He scowls a bit. "I'm busting my butt twenty-four hours a day for these dick-heads."

Diane touches his face, rubbing the sparse whiskers on his chin. "You're an animal, baby. Don't let 'em get to you."

"I won't."

"You sleep," she says. "I'll come by for you some-time. Around eight. Maybe I'll even bake you some cookies."

"Great," he says flatly. "I gotta get out of here before I punch somebody."

She flexes her arms. "I'd hit back," she teases.

He walks off, down the hill toward the school. Then he hears Reed calling him. He's standing by his car in the lot behind the track.

"Come here!" he yells.

Herbie lets out a sigh. *This is all I need,* he thinks. But he walks over.

"What?" Herbie says.

"You been thinking about what I said?"

"About what?"

"You know. The ladies. Want to pull a little switcheroo tonight? You take a shot at Ellie and let me go with Diane?"

"Man, you are such a shit-head," Herbie says. "Why the hell would I do that?"

"Come on. I can set it up."

"Bull*shit*. You can not. You're an asshole, you know that?"

Reed gives him a little shove. "Watch your mouth."

"You watch *your* mouth, dick." Herbie shoves back.

Reed steps up real close now, right in Herbie's face. "What are you, some hot-shit football star now? I'll kick your ass, pal."

"I don't think so," Herbie says.

"I do."

"It'd take me about two seconds, asshole." Herbie puts his hand up on Reed's chest now, not shoving, but applying some pressure. He's taken more than enough shit this morning, and he's ready to fight.

Reed swings his forearm toward Herbie's head, but Herbie blocks it and grabs the other arm. He punches Reed in the chest, and Reed comes back with a fist that catches Herbie in the cheek.

They wrestle to the pavement, and Herbie gets the advantage, connecting with a couple of punches to the shoulders before the coach and two other runners yank them apart.

"Enough, enough, enough!" Coach says. "What is wrong with you guys?" He points at Herbie. "Didn't I just warn you about your attitude? You come out here and start acting like a hyena?"

"He started it," Herbie says.

"Bullshit!" Reed says. "The jerk came after me." Reed wipes his knee with his palm, flicking off some blood. "Asshole. Jumping me on the pavement."

The coach looks at Reed, then at Herbie. "Reed," he says, "I saw you call him over. Don't bullshit me.

"As for you," he says to Herbie, "consider this your first and only warning. You're *this* close"—he holds his thumb and fingertip a quarter-inch apart—"to being off the team. Now both of you get out of here. I get word that anything else happens this weekend, and I'll can both your butts. You got that, Reed?"

"Yeah."

Coach starts to walk away. He beckons Herbie with his finger. Herbie goes over.

"Learn how to channel it, my friend. You hear me?"

"Yeah."

"No more negatives. You have to make that anger work for you. Don't let a guy like Reed jerk you around. You've got more heart than he does."

Herbie stares at him. This guy is giving him a compliment? He lets out his breath. "Okay," he says. "I got ya."

"You played well last night," he says. "More than I can say for the rest of your squad."

"We got whipped."

"Like I said, on this team we hand out most of the beatings. Think real hard about running full-time."

"I'll think about it," he says. But he won't do it. Not this season. "I'll think about it, Coach," he says again. "But I think I got too much in my head already."

Chapter Twenty-One

Herbie eats a shit-load of food from the refrigerator: a carton of leftover fried rice from the Chinese place, a container of blueberry yogurt, a handful of square slices of orange cheese, three ice-cream sandwiches, and a Sprite, and then he takes a nap. Then he logs on to the Internet.

Who goes into a physics chat room on a Saturday afternoon? Not many people. The diehards. He reads the recent postings about quarks, time warps, and wormholes in space. Then he sends a one-word instant message to cosmo-not: afterlife?

cosmo-not *8/31 14:27* What about it?

goalie *8/31 14:28* Think any more about it?

cosmo-not *8/31 14:28* Yeah. Why do you ask?

goalie *8/31 14:29* I had a conversation with my brother last night.

cosmo-not *8/31 14:29* Your dead brother?

goalie *8/31 14:29* Yeah. Not exactly a conversation. I talked. He was there. He heard me.

cosmo-not *8/31 14:30* Kule. Where did this take place?

goalie *8/31 14:30* Right at his grave. I think we're getting closer. I really felt like he heard me.

cosmo-not *8/31 14:31* So now what?

goalie *8/31 14:31* I could see the other ghost clearer each time I encountered him. So I'm thinking the same might happen with Frank. I'm going back there tonight with my girlfriend. I'll let you know what happens.

cosmo-not *8/31 14:32* Yeah. Let me know. I'll be on after midnight your time.

goalie *8/31 14:32* Your time is different?

cosmo-not *8/31 14:32* I'm in Calgary. Home of the Stampede. We're two hours behind you.

goalie *8/31 14:33* Oh. Must be cold.

cosmo-not *8/31 14:33* Not in summer. Duh. Got a question for you. You think we can come back after death? Not as ghosts, but to live over?

goalie *8/31 14:34* Reincarnation. Like I've said, I think anything is possible. Yeah, why not? I think it happens sometimes. Not to most people.

cosmo-not *8/31 14:34* I kind of hope so. Life's too short.

goalie *8/31 14:35* I hear you. Listen, I gotta run. Literally. I need a workout. Clear my head.

cosmo-not *8/31 14:35* Go for it. Talk to you later.

Chapter Twenty-Two

Diane shows up at about ten minutes to eight in an olive-colored tank top, low-cut jeans, and her sandals. Our mom is surprised to see a girl at the door asking for Herbie, but she smiles and lets her in.

"I'm Diane. Herbie must have told you about me?"

"Well, not really," Mom says. "Herbie," she calls. "*Diane* is here to see you."

"Okay," he calls down the stairs.

Mom is looking her over. They both look happy. Herbie comes trotting down the stairs. "What's up?" he says.

"I brought a movie," Diane says, holding up a case. "And cookies."

Mom smiles at Herbie and gives him a raised-eyebrow look, like *Why didn't you mention this?* She'll grill him later, but she's obviously pleased.

The movie is *The Haunting*. "Thought we'd raise some goose bumps," Diane says. "Ever see this?"

"Yeah," he says. "Once."

"Want to watch it with us, Mrs. Herbert?"

"Thanks. But I'll leave you guys alone. I will have a cookie, though."

They sit on the couch in the living room and put in the tape. "So, what do you think?" Diane asks.

"About what?"

She raises her eyebrows. "You didn't notice anything different?"

"Like what?"

Now she rolls her eyes and sighs. She lifts her foot and wiggles it at him.

"What?" he says.

"I painted my *toenails,*" she says.

"Ohhhhhh. Yeah," he says. "Yeah. They look great."

She smacks his arm. "You didn't even notice. You butt-head."

They watch the movie and make out during a lot of it. He tells her about his encounter with me last night.

"You want to go back tonight?" she asks.

"Yeah."

"Let's go."

"We can wait till the movie's over."

"Okay."

The moon is not up yet, so it is considerably dark as they walk along River Road. They stop when they get inside the cemetery, and he bends his head back to look at the universe.

"Look how huge that is," he whispers. "Every one of those stars is so far away from us. We're like this insignificant speck down here. All you have to do is look up there at night, and you know how incredible this whole existence is."

"It's amazing," she says. She runs her hand over his back, squeezing the muscles as she goes.

"You can't tell me we're alone in all this," he says. "That there aren't others out there who think and create. Gotta be life out there. Lots of it."

They walk along slowly. "Herbie?" she says after a few minutes.

"Yeah?"

"What's your name?"

"My real name?"

"Yeah. It isn't Herbie Herbert?"

He laughs. "No. It's Warren. Nobody's called me that since about second grade. Even my parents."

"Warren Herbert." She pokes his arm and makes a scrunched-up face at him. "Little Warren Herbert," she says in a teasing way. She kisses him on the mouth. "We should have brought a blanket," she says.

"Would have been nice."

"We'll make do," she says. She takes his hand and leads him toward the hill, up toward those slate steps again.

I watch from a distance for a few minutes, the flashes of orange, the giggling. Then I leave them be. They'll find me later, I'm certain.

I approach that corner of the cemetery where Eamon is buried, that little gully where he often appears. I have noticed that his resemblance to me and to Herbie is striking. He looks like teenage pictures of my father and my grandfather. You know how you see a picture of someone you've never seen before and you just know, "That *has* to be a Kennedy" or "That kid *must* be one of the Fowlers." Grampa told me that *his* grandfather—my great-great-grandfather—was a bastard child, never knew his father. Born to a shopkeeper right here in Sturbridge. Could have been Gwen the prostitute, couldn't it? Could have been Eamon's own baby. That would explain the connection with Herbie.

"Eamon," I say. "Can you hear me?"

I feel myself drifting; the space gets colder. There is a foul aroma, a taste of rotting leaves and of dampness. The scenery fades, and I am on a mistier level, still here in the cemetery but less substantive. And Eamon is before me, bright but transparent. He is staring at me. He doesn't speak.

"I'm Frank," I say. "I think you're my ancestor. Can you hear me?"

He blinks and nods slightly. His expression is of confusion, of fear, of helplessness.

"What are you searching for?" I ask him. "Do you know?" I look around. I can just make out the trees and the path and the gravestones. They are blurry and in motion. Only Eamon is clear to me.

"You've been dead a lot of years," I say. "You've been wandering in here like you're lost and bewildered. There's got to be a way out, Eamon."

Eamon winces a little, backs away.

"I've been stuck, too," I tell him. "I haven't let go. Maybe that's all it takes, though. Maybe we just have to let go."

Eamon flickers a little, gets brighter, then fades. He shakes his head at me, finally shows a bit of recognition. "Bring him here," he says.

"Bring who?" I ask.

"Bring who?" he replies.

"I just asked you that."

"I just asked you that."

"Stop playing games."

"Stop playing games."

I blink. He blinks. And it occurs to me that he is not playing, not simply mimicking me. It is as if I am looking in a mirror. Like I am looking deep into my past.

I wait by my grave. *At rest.* How ironic. I look at those stars Herbie was pondering. This universe is vast. I used to think that when we died we'd suddenly know all the answers, that all those mysteries about God and creation and other intelligences would be revealed to us; we'd know about angels and black holes and kryptonite and the Loch Ness monster, and we'd get to meet Plato and da Vinci and see Elvis perform.

And that our physical desires would cease.

Not quite. It's all there for us, and we've got eternity to explore it, but the initiative still has to come from each one of us. I'm no closer to the stars than I've ever been.

What's another hundred years for Eamon? Hell, what's another million? We all progress at our own rates. Maybe, in some way I can't quite comprehend, parts of the same soul even progress at different rates from each other. The trick is to have them catch up, to re-merge.

Herbie and Diane are walking toward my grave now. Herbie is telling her how we used to play checkers and electric football. They look great together, so happy and in tune. There has to be some equivalent connection possible in the afterlife, doesn't there?

"Frank took me to the movies almost every Saturday," Herbie says. "He couldn't have liked the movies; cartoony crap about baby dinosaurs and wizards. He just liked being with me."

They sit on the ground on the spongy moss a few feet from the grave. She sits cross-legged with her hand on his knee. He sits with his legs straight out, less flexible than she is. They talk to each other, and Herbie makes occasional references to me. "Remember that, Frank?" he says, or "Diane's into Dylan, too, buddy. She loves that song 'Shooting Star.'"

After a few minutes Herbie starts laughing. "Oh, man. I just remembered a great one," he says. "Diane, we had this dumb game called Pony Polo. You got down on your hands and knees and put these straps around your head to secure a plastic hockey-stick thing to your forehead, and you had to move your head back and forth to hit a little foam ball. It was like field hockey, but we played it in the living room."

"One on one?" she says.

Herbie starts laughing so hard he can't even speak, but I know what he wants to say next. He finally gets it out. "Yeah. One on one. But we had this stupid-ass song that we made ourselves sing the whole time we played the game," he says. He doubles over. Tears are coming out of his eyes, he's laughing so hard. "So we're down on all fours, whacking this ball around with these headpieces, and we're singing, 'We *plaaaaay* the game of Pony *Po*-lo. We *plaaaaay* the game of Pony *Po*-lo.' We sing that same monotonous line over and over, like a thousand times during the game. You get a penalty if you stop singing! And we know how ridiculous it is. That's the whole idea."

Diane is laughing, too. "That's so sweet," she says.

"It was hilarious." He wipes his eyes. "It was classic. Where'd we come up with that stuff, Frank? It was like it came out of both of us, you know? Like two heads were better than one."

Diane does not speak directly to me, but I think she believes that I'm here. Seems like she's doing more than just humoring my brother. But I don't need to interact with her. I'll wait till he comes back alone.

I don't have to wait long. He walks her home and returns within an hour, having stopped at the house for a sweatshirt and a bottle of Rolling Rock.

"Frankie, you remember those big-ass boxing gloves we found in Grampa's attic?" he says. "You taught me how to fight with them on. You started showing me how to defend myself, and I whacked you in the jaw. Funny shit."

It was. What a ball of energy Herbie was when he was little. He'd come at me in those boxing gloves with his fists flying—I'd be on my knees—and all I could do was cover my head and laugh. Tough kid, but we loved each other completely.

I can feel myself smiling now, happier than I've been in years. I try to sing. "We *plaaaaay*—" Herbie stares at me, his mouth open in astonishment. I stare back. I start to sing again, and he joins in "the game of Pony *Po*-lo."

"Holy shit, Frank," says Herbie, and he stands and takes a step toward me. He reaches out his hand, and I reach back, but there is nothing physical between us. "My God, Frank," he says. "I knew it, man. I knew it. You've been with me all these years, and I knew it."

And suddenly I feel an exhaustion, an inability to

do anything but watch him and listen to him. For a second I was visible, he was staring right at me. I crossed into his realm. Now I feel totally spent. I glance around and I'm on the misty level again; the physical parts of the cemetery are cloudy, and I feel that I am drifting. Eamon is nearby, staring at me hard but not speaking.

Herbie looks at my grave. Whispers to me. "Where are you, Frank?"

I'm here.

Chapter Twenty-Three

Sunday afternoons are slow at the diner, so it's just Herbie and Kevin in the kitchen. Tomorrow is Labor Day; school starts the next day, and on Wednesday there's a cross-country race at home against Milford.

Kevin's been asking about the ghost situation, but Herbie is noncommittal. "So the guy just disappeared?" Kevin asks. He's asking about Eamon; Kevin doesn't know about Herbie's connection with me.

"I don't know. I haven't seen him since that night he fell off the cliff." Herbie's at the sink scrubbing a giant roasting pan. Kevin's loading the dishwasher. "Your grandmother said they run out of energy sometimes and lie there dormant. The guy probably just lost steam. Who knows?"

"There's plenty of others in there," Kevin says. "That cemetery is Ghost Central."

"Yeah," Herbie says. "I've seen some other activity."

But he doesn't say what. He tries to change the subject to the Yankees.

"They say there's ghosts in there that'll crush your testicles if you get near 'em," Kevin says.

"Now why would they do that?"

"Just viciousness," he says. "I swear to God."

Herbie shakes his head. "I don't think so," he says. "I think that happened in *The Exorcist.* These ghosts aren't vindictive or anything. They're just lost. They're drifters."

"Maybe the ones you run into are, but there are psychos in there, believe me. They'll slit your frickin' throat. I ain't kidding."

Herbie laughs a little, sets a soapy pot on the side of the sink. "Good stories," he says. "Scary. But I don't think it's like that in there. It's a pretty peaceful place in my experience."

"You've just been lucky," Kevin says.

"Yeah," Herbie answers. "I have."

After work Herbie walks over to our dad's house. The NFL season started today; Dad's watching the Chargers against the Rams.

"Evening, Chief," Dad says. "How's life at the diner?"

"Not bad. Not bad."

"Giants got their asses kicked today."

"Not any worse than we did, I expect."

Dad laughs. "I think you guys found a running back, at least, if your coach is smart enough to play you."

Herbie shrugs. "I don't know. I may have been the fastest guy on the field, but Pocono had like the next twenty fastest. That might be the worst we get beat on all season. At least until Berwick, I guess."

Dad moves some stuff off the couch next to him: a giant bag of potato chips, a couple of empty beer cans, an ashtray. "Sit down, Idjit."

"Sure. Any score yet?"

"Seven–zip, Chargers. You working tomorrow?"

"Nah. You?"

"Nope. Even those pricks don't make us work on Labor Day."

"I got a race on Wednesday," Herbie says. "Can you get there?"

"Home?"

"Yeah."

"I'll try. Pretty good chance, I think."

Herbie looks around the room, which is relatively neat for our father. The Sunday newspaper is stacked in three different places, and the TV insert is on the floor by the couch, so the place looks lived in but not trashed.

"Dad?"

"Yeah?"

Herbie lets out his breath and looks up at the ceiling. "Dad, you think about Frank much?"

Dad is quiet for a few seconds. He takes a swig of beer. "Yup," he says finally. "I think about him every single day. Poor bastard."

"Yeah. Me, too."

"Real kick in the ass for a guy to die so young," Dad says. "I would have traded places in a second. Would do it for you, too. If it was possible."

"I know, Dad." Herbie watches the television for a minute as the Rams punter kicks one toward the corner of the field, where it rolls dead inside the five.

"I think he's okay, Dad."

"Think so?"

"Yeah, I do. I think he knows, you know, how we're doing. And I think he's in a good place. I think so."

Dad nods slowly, staring at the set. "I like to think so," he says. He looks over at Herbie, gives him a tight-lipped smile. "I guess we'll find out someday, huh? Either we will or we won't. And if we don't, then it doesn't really matter. If we're dead when we die, then we'll never know it."

"Yeah," Herbie says. "I guess that's true." I can tell he's reluctant to talk more about this, to share what he knows with Dad. Maybe later; maybe he's just planting the seed.

"I think Frank's okay, though," Herbie says again. "I really have a good feeling about him."

When Herbie gets back to Mom's house, he has this E-mail from cosmo-not in Calgary, sent earlier in the evening:

Hey buster. Been thinking. I'm just throwing this out there, not to burst your bubble. But who's allowed in this afterlife of yours, anyway? Cro-Magnons? Neanderthals? They were human--they must have had souls, right? So do you have a population of grunting tool-users up there in Heaven? What about pre-humans, way back in evolution? Hell, do dolphins get there? Mosquitos? Where do you draw the line of soul vs. matter? How exclusive is this club of yours? Are there dinosaurs bumping around up there?

He responds with an instant message.

goalie *9/1 21:27* Good questions. (You a little grumpy today dude?) You know I don't have any answers. Don't some religions say we keep coming back, living new, more advanced lives each time, until we're finally ready to move toward Nirvana? So you could have been a mosquito back in the Cretaceous, then a lizard, then a monkey, then a caveman a million years ago, and a peasant building the pyramids, before becoming a rodeo fan up in the Yukon.

cosmo-not *9/1 21:29* Calgary's in Alberta. OK. Convenient answer. No, I'm not grumpy. Just a bit fatalistic today. So reincarnation is a big part of your theory?

goalie *9/1 21:30* Guess so. It fills in some little gaps in the plan, doesn't it?

cosmo-not *9/1 21:30* I guess we can explain anything if we try hard enough. Doesn't mean it's true.

goalie *9/1 21:31* Never said it was. Maybe this whole thing is in my head. But you can't explain away my brother. I was with him last night. He was SINGING!

cosmo-not *9/1 21:32* Get it on tape.

goalie *9/1 21:32* You can fake anything with tape. No one would believe it. I don't need to share it. You can discount it if you want to. Hell, you have to have doubt. I could be a hoaxter. I know I'm not, but all you have to go by is what I tell you.

cosmo-not *9/1 21:33* No. I think you're on to something. I do. I don't know what it is, but you certainly believe what you're telling me.

cosmo-not *9/1 21:35* You still there?

goalie *9/1 21:35* Yeah. Just thinking.

cosmo-not *9/1 21:36* What was he singing?

goalie *9/1 21:36* Just this dumb song we made up when I was little. Pretty funny.

cosmo-not *9/1 21:37* Very cool.

goalie *9/1 21:37* Yeah. Listen, I'm tired as hell. I need to go for a run and then crash. Talk to you later.

Chapter Twenty-Four

Last night in a dream state I found myself in the 1880s, when the town of Sturbridge was still known as Dyberry Forks. I had the same yearnings and frustrations that I have now, but in my dream I was alive and physical. I could clench my fists, could feel the rain on my face, and feel smoke stinging my eyes.

In my dream I knew fear and I knew desire. I tasted the warm, salty aroma of a woman's naked skin, felt the slick, gripping texture of her as I wriggled and churned, felt the height of approaching orgasm and the sustained power of its release, felt all of this from deep within my memory, from a place so ingrained in me that it seemed to extend to my very beginning.

In my dream I knew the labor of a dark, rainy climb up the cliff, grunting with effort as I grasped at bushes and boulders and hauled myself up the slope. I knew the tension in my fingertips as I slowly climbed the final feet toward the top of the steepest face, knew the sudden panic of a fatal misstep, felt the astonished, slow-motion drop through space and the flattening impact of the crash.

I wait in Herbie's room while he runs, looking at his CDs. Not a lot of new stuff; Herbie is into Dylan and Springsteen and the Grateful Dead. I look in on Mom one last time, reading in bed. Lots of pictures of us boys in her room.

Herbie showers and lies down on his bed with the light on, listening to *Blood on the Tracks.*

"Hey," I say.

He looks up and sees me. Blinks hard. "Hey."

"Come to the cemetery with me?" I ask.

"Sure." He stares at me while pulling on his pants and shoes, never taking his eyes from me.

"You all right?" I ask.

"Tired," he says. "Guess I'm not asleep, though. Am I?"

I laugh. "Nah. You're awake," I say. "It's me. Rejuvenated."

"Jesus," he says. He's staring with his mouth open. "Where've you been, Frank?"

"Around."

"Around here?"

"Yeah," I say. "Earth. The air. This huge dark space out there. I can go anywhere, but it scares the shit out of me. If I went much farther, I don't think I could come back."

There's a knock on the bedroom door.

"Herbie?" It's Mom.

"Yeah."

"Who are you talking to?"

"Just thinking out loud, Ma."

"Oh." She opens the door and peeks in. She looks around the room and smiles at Herbie. I say hello, but she does not hear me or see me. She says, "See you in the morning," to Herbie. "School starts, remember." She shuts the door.

Herbie looks at me, sitting here as plain as day. He points toward the door, raises his eyebrows a bit. "How come *I* can see you?" he asks.

"Because I'm here."

"How come I've never been able to see you till now, Frank? Or hear you?"

"I don't know," I say. "I think you weren't perceptive enough. I think I wasn't either."

He leaves his bedroom, walks down the stairs, and steps outside, and I follow him down the block.

"So what's up?" he says as he crosses Main Street, trusting that I'm still with him.

"Transition time." And when I say it, I get a cold rush, like the halting of your breath at a moment of crucial decision.

Herbie's quiet until we reach River Road and approach the cemetery, where it's dark and there are no houses and he can whisper aloud without anyone to hear. At the gate he stops and looks around. When he sees me, he reaches out his hand. I reach back.

"So," he says, "you been *between* things for a while, huh?"

"Yeah," I say. "I've been stuck. And scared."

He nods. "But you're over it?"

"Getting there," I say. I look him over—his face, his hands, his substance. "I'm still scared."

"Was that you in my dreams, Frank? Did you visit me when I was asleep?"

"Yeah. Lots of times. Sometimes I was dreaming, too." I have a sudden, funny thought. "Remember that song we made up after that cowboy-boot incident?" I say.

He smiles. "Definitely."

I sing it. Two verses that repeat over and over: "Hey, smelly dog, how are you today? You smell like doo, and you're eatin' hay, hey, hey! Hey, smelly dog, how are you right now? You smell like doo, and I stepped in cow, hey, hey!"

Herbie's got a big smile. "Brilliant lyrics," he says.

"Yeah. What talent."

We enter the cemetery, and he walks along the path. The breeze is cool. "I read what that Canadian was saying," I say. "About reincarnation."

"Oh yeah?"

"Yeah. Interesting."

"You think?"

"Yeah," I say. "I've thought about it from time to time. It happens. You just have to suspend who you are for a while. I think you make the choice on your own, but then you don't remember anything about your previous lives until you die again. That seems to be part of the deal."

"Oh."

"See, you've wondered if I've been stuck in limbo, and in a way, I have been. I know this sounds really greedy, but there are too many things I missed out on. So the choice to move forward isn't one I've been big on. What I've really always wanted is to go *back*."

"As someone else?"

"Yes and no. The circumstances would be different. I might wind up in Brazil or Algeria or *Scranton*. But it would be me, essentially. I just wouldn't really know it, I suppose. Until I died again and could look back."

"Yeah." He gives me a serious look. "What are you

missing, Frank? What can't you go on without getting?"

I think for a second for a way to put it. "A personal connection," I say. "Kind of what you're developing with Diane. Not just sex, but something deeper. Sex, too. But love. I need love on a physical level. You know what I'm saying? I need it."

"Of course I know, Frank. Man, of course I get it. Until I met Diane I was always on the edge. I know what you're saying, man. I know it."

"Well, I'll be moving on soon, brother. This isn't the end, though, you hear me?"

"Yeah, Frank."

"Listen," I say. "Sometime you'll find a way to help Mom and Dad understand this. Do me a favor and try."

"I will. I started with Dad a little."

"I know. That's good. There's no way they'd ever be receptive enough to see me. Just give them a little assurance when you can. Mom's almost ready, I think. It won't upset her to know that you think about me."

"I will."

I listen to the breeze for a minute or so. "Herbie," I finally say. "I feel like I've been through this before. This whole death thing. It's like I'm going through it twice at the same time."

"What do you mean?"

"Just this feeling that I've been through this before.

This inability to move on. Like it happened to me in another life. I mean, in another *death,* if you know what I'm saying."

"Déjà vu?"

"All over again."

Herbie looks toward the treetops, rubs his eyes lightly with his fingertips. "Who's that other ghost, Frank?" he asks. "The one I keep running into. The guy who looks like us?"

"His name is Eamon," I say. I nod my head slowly. "He *is* one of us, Herbie."

"Like a relative?"

"Yeah. Just like one. Five, six generations back." I make a swirling motion with my finger. "It's all circular," I tell him. "Everything comes back to where it started. . . . Come on."

"Where to?"

"To find him."

"Why?"

"Just this feeling I have. The three of us need to be together. It's time to resolve this thing."

Eamon is not hard to find. He is at the base of the path that leads to the cliff, glowing more brightly than I've seen him.

"Sucker always startles me," Herbie says.

"He's not all there."

"Yeah. Obviously."

"No. I mean . . . what you're seeing is just a fraction of who he was. That's just his fear and his frustration. The rest of him made it through. But he could never quite rest in either place—in the afterlife or back on Earth."

"Shit."

"I know why now. And I know how to fix it."

Eamon turns and is climbing the cliff, as he's tried to do a thousand times over the years. I start to follow.

"Tough climb," Herbie says.

"Yeah," I say. "But essential."

Herbie sticks his hands in the pouch of his sweat-shirt, making no move to start climbing. "He always falls, doesn't he?" Herbie asks.

"So far," I answer. "Something was missing, though. I think we finally found it."

He nods and looks up at Eamon. I have to get going.

"You leaving me, Frank?" he asks.

"In a way," I say, "yeah."

"Thanks for sticking by me," he says.

"It's been worth it," I tell him.

"I'll see you again, Frank. I love ya."

"I love you too, brother," I say.

He wipes his eye; his voice is choked. "I wish I could hug you," he says.

"You can," I tell him. "Step toward me."

I lean in and he shuts his eyes. "I'm still vital," I whisper. "You feel that warmth, man? That's me."

"Yeah," he says. "I feel it."

"That doesn't burn out, Herbie. Nothing can kill it. You'll keep part of me with you forever."

"I feel it, Frank. And I'll keep it."

I step back, take a look up the hill, and whisper, "It's time now."

"I know, brother. I love you."

"I love you, too," I tell him. "Keep the shit off your boots."

"You got it."

Eamon is looking at me with anticipation now, glancing back to make sure that I am following. He stares at me hard, turns and climbs a few feet, and turns back and stares some more, checking on my progress.

I'm remembering things as I climb. Times I'd walk into a store on Main Street and know that I'd been there before—not a week ago or last year, but *a hundred* years ago or more. Back in the 1880s, when there were Civil War vets hanging around town and the shop that now sells sporting goods and sneakers was Olaf M. Spettigue's Store, the walls lined with hardware and farming tools, or when the gift shop next to Rite Aid was the home of Guckenberger's City Boot & Shoe Store. When canal workers drank the nights away at the Dyberry Tavern. When the streets were rutted mud, and horses were the mode of transportation. When Gwen the shopkeeper let me into her body.

I remember the taste of whiskey, which never passed my lips in my seventeen years as Frank, and the smell and sounds of the canal.

I feel the loose grittiness of the pebbles as I climb in the gully, smell the damp leaves and the soil, hear the soft gushing of the river down below.

As a kid I always had a chill when I was up on top of the cliff, always a knot in my gut when I climbed around on the ledges beneath the steepest grade. Always an irrational feeling that I'd suddenly lose my footing and fall.

In death, I've avoided this spot. Only once have I been here, when I followed Herbie and Eamon on that night Eamon fell again, when I experienced that falling with him, knew that desperation of the plunge toward death, felt that bone-crunching impact when his body hit the earth.

In life I always had a gap within my soul, some

missing element from my past. Some derailment had occurred; some part of me got left behind.

In death I've always wondered, *Why did I die so young?*

And now I'm left wondering, *Why has it happened to me twice?*

We're nearing the top now, inching our way up, searching carefully for crevices in which to wedge my feet, feeling the brittle rock with my fingers to find a firm spot to grip. I was Eamon, then I was transience, then I was nothing but energy, and then I became Frank. And somehow the part of me that never caught up, that lost bit of soul that stayed in the Dyberry Cemetery and smoldered with Eamon's body, eventually reignited and sought frantically to rejoin me. To connect to me through Herbie—his brother, his great-great-great-grandson, the most physically kinesthetic soul to ever run through our graveyard.

I have caught up to Eamon and am overtaking him, my body actually merging into his, rejoining the part I've been missing. The part that went back to its own desperate search. The part of me that fell from this cliff.

A final strong handhold and I am clawing over the steepest ledge, pulling us up and over the top, my knee finding firm rock to kneel on, my other leg scrambling up as well. His fingers in the dirt. My fingers. I lunge forward, onto flat ground, and stand and look down at the town and feel suddenly whole again. It's been a long time since I felt this way. A blink of the eye. More than a century. Barely a breath. An eternity.

All of me is present. My past is present.

Eamon and Frank are one again.

Epilogue

Herbie ran well in his first cross-country race, finishing as sixth man for Sturbridge and eighth overall. The football team lost again later in the week, 37–0, and Herbie carried four times for nineteen yards and missed a thirty-eight-yard field goal attempt.

From there, the cross-country team won its next three dual meets and placed third in the Scranton Invitational, with Herbie maintaining his spot as sixth or seventh man on the varsity.

The football team finally turned things around against Midvale, winning in dramatic fashion when Herbie booted a seventeen-yard field goal as time expired, for a 9–7 victory.

I have gone back and forth from the earthly realm to the next one for several weeks. I've been waiting for one last autumn day, one classic afternoon of turning leaves and crisp clean air and apples ripening and beautiful girls in sweaters.

It isn't so easy—reincarnation—but I'm moving in that direction again. There are lessons I have to learn on my level of the afterlife first, issues I have to confront. It's not like you just go down to the draft board and sign up for a hitch in another body. But it *is* an option, and I am thinking I might take it. I could try to move forward in the afterlife, but I'd feel like one of those too-smart twelve-year-olds who winds up in college or med school. Don't they need to be a kid first before they become an adult? I need to be a man before becoming a spirit. I've gotten derailed too early in two different lifetimes, one time as Eamon and one time as Frank.

Herbie's team is racing against Laurelton today, their most significant rival for league supremacy. Laurelton had won three straight titles before Sturbridge edged them out last season. Both teams are undefeated in dual meets this fall.

Cross-country, despite being a sport of individual effort, is also very definitely a team sport. One guy can't carry a team alone. The first five runners on each team score, with one point for first, two for second, etc. Lowest total score of each team's top five runners wins. Today's meet is one where the fourth and fifth men may be decisive.

They are out on the course, and the coach is hollering as the runners race past the track, heading for the final loop through the woods. Herbie's teammate Ron is way out in front, but Laurelton has second and third. Two from each team are battling for the next spots, and Herbie is in the following pack, running as Sturbridge's fifth man with less than a mile to go.

"This is the meet right here, guys!" the coach yells as Herbie's group races past. "This is what'll decide it!"

Herbie passes a Laurelton runner on the final hill and charges toward the next one on the dirt path through the woods. He is in tenth place as they approach the track for the final hundred meters, no more than three yards back of the fifth Laurelton runner. With four runners in from both teams, they are tied at 18–18. If Herbie can catch this guy, they'll win it by a point. If he can't, then Laurelton wins.

I'm betting on Herbie. I can see him digging down, reaching for that open-field speed that makes him a threat in football. Diane and the other girls and the runners who've finished are screaming at him to kick.

"This is it, Herbie!" Diane's yelling, jumping up and down at the side of the track. "This is everything!"

He is a stride behind with fifty meters left, clawing with his arms, his eyes and mouth open wide in a grimace, legs pumping furiously. He pulls even but not ahead, and they bump elbows and scramble to the finish line.

Herbie finishes inches ahead and raises his fists in triumph. The Laurelton guy collapses to the ground. Herbie closes his eyes and sucks in air, feeling the pain. His teammates are going wild.

Herbie is hugging Diane, so thrilled to have made a big impact on the race. It wasn't always easy, but life is like that. Sometimes death is, too.

My little brother, Herbie. So bright, so funny, so very, very physical. I'll miss the guy, but that'll be temporary. Time is on our side.

After all, we have all the time in the universe. Our paths are finally clear.

Rich Wallace is the author of *Wrestling Sturbridge*, an ALA Top Ten Best Book for Young Adults, and *Shots on Goal* and *Playing Without the Ball*, both *Booklist* Top Ten Best Youth Sports Books. He's worked as a sportswriter, a news editor, and a magazine editor. He lives with his wife and two sons in northeastern Pennsylvania.